We Still Belong

ALSO BY CHRISTINE DAY

I Can Make This Promise
The Sea in Winter
She Persisted: Maria Tallchief

We Still Belong

CHRISTINE DAY

Heartdrum
An Imprint of HarperCollins Publishers

Heartdrum is an imprint of HarperCollins Publishers.

We Still Belong

Library of Congress Cataloging-in-Publication Data

Names: Day, Christine, 1993– author.
Title: We still belong / Christine Day.
Description: First edition. | New York : Heartdrum, an imprint of
     HarperCollins Publishers, [2023] | Audience: Ages 8–12. | Audience:
     Grades 4–6. | Summary: "Wesley's hopeful plans for Indigenous
     Peoples' Day (and asking her crush to the dance) go all wrong—until
     she finds herself surrounded by the love of her Indigenous family and
     community at the intertribal powwow"— Provided by publisher.
Identifiers: LCCN 2022031730 | ISBN 9780063064560 (hardcover)
Subjects: CYAC: Identity—Fiction. | Interpersonal relations—Fiction. |
     Family relations—Fiction.
Classification: LCC PZ7.1.D392 We 2023 | DDC [Fic]—dc23
LC record available at https://lccn.loc.gov/2022031730

Typography by Sarah Nichole Kaufman and Celeste Knudsen
23 24 25 26 27 LBC 5 4 3 2 1

First Edition

For the kids who yearn to belong.

And in memory of Caesar, who had the bluest eyes,
the softest meows, and the sharpest claws.

1

Indigenous Peoples' Day—*Paciłtalbixw tiʔəʔ sləx̌il*

It's early in the morning and I'm curled up on the couch, finishing a homework assignment for my health class while Vader purrs near my ear. He slinks along the windowsill beside me and stretches, extending his front claws, lifting his tail high, curling it into the shape of a hook. His eyes are bright green. His fur is short and sleek and black, except for a little white patch on his chest.

He stares at me, one ear flicking irritably, waiting to be acknowledged.

I set my pencil aside and stroke the top of his head. Satisfied, Vader nuzzles against my hand, his purrs deepening with each exhale.

"Couldn't sleep, boy?" I whisper. Vader blinks at me slowly. "Yeah. Me neither."

I barely slept at all.

Everyone else is still snoozing upstairs. Even Baby Zoe seems to be sleeping through the night, and she's *teething* right now.

Not me. I was restless, constantly tossing and turning. I kept staring at the ceiling, at the numbers on the alarm clock, at the back of my mother's head. Her bed is across the room from mine. She had a sleep mask drawn over her eyes; her dark hair was tucked into a long braid that snaked across her silk pillowcase. I could hear Grandpa's wheezing snore from two doors down the hall. And just after two a.m., I was awake and aware of Auntie Jess when she came home from her shift at the hospital. I listened to her careful, measured footsteps as she crept up the stairs and past our door on her way to the room she shared with Uncle Kenji, with Baby Zoe's bassinet at their bedside.

Eventually, I realized sleep wouldn't come to me; I figured that I might as well finish my homework while the house was still and quiet.

I snuck out of bed and down the stairs.

The sun hadn't risen, so I switched on the floor lamp; it bathed everything in a warm amber glow, illuminating the moss-green couches, the golden-brown floorboards, the gently curved wicker chairs around the dining table. A bookcase consumes an entire living room wall, filled with bird-watching guides, carved wooden figurines, science fiction novels, and laminated family albums. The TV is mounted in the middle of the opposite wall, a great and gleaming black mirror. The shelves beneath it hold boxy bins full of video game equipment, plus a tin popcorn bucket that doesn't fit anywhere in the kitchen. Baskets full of colorful blocks and rolled-up burping cloths for Baby Zoe are tucked away in the corners of the room, along with scratching posts for Vader.

Vader reaches over me now, still purring, all lean and soft and warm, innocently flexing his paw. Then—*quick*—he bats at my pencil, sending it skittering across the floor.

I give him a look. "You did that on purpose."

Vader flicks his whiskers. Keeps on purring.

"You're lucky you're so cute," I tell him.

I flop over the edge of the couch, reaching for the pencil—it has rolled all the way over to my backpack, which is beside my stickered viola case by the front door. Ready for Monday. For school. For today.

My palms go clammy. There's a reason why I was tossing and turning all night. A reason why I could barely close my eyes.

And that reason is a boy. His name is Ryan.

2

Well, okay. He's not the *only* reason. I'm just jittery about everything that is set to happen at school today. This is going to be a big day for me. A day of firsts.

I'm going to have my first piece published in the school newspaper—a poem about Indigenous Peoples' Day. It's personal and meaningful and important to me, as a descendant of the Upper Skagit Indian Tribe. I also think it's better than any English assignment I've ever turned in. I'm proud and nervous and excited and scared to see it in print. My stomach does somersaults whenever I think about my classmates reading it.

So far, the only people who have read it are my best friend, Hanan—since she is one of the newspaper's editors, and the whole thing was sort of her idea—and Ms. Roux, the language arts teacher who oversees the production of the *Shorelands Times*. Then my mom begged to read it. She and Auntie Jess and Uncle Kenji and Grandpa all teamed up and convinced me to read the poem aloud at the dinner table, while they listened and nodded, their brown eyes all bright with pride. Mom even wept a little bit—she's sentimental like that. And by the end of it, they all whistled and cheered, chanting my name as I blushed and cringed away from their attention. It was loud and silly and embarrassing, but I was grateful. My family made me feel like I'd done something big. Something significant.

I wonder what my English teacher will think of it. Mr. Holt awards extra-credit points to his students whose columns are selected for the school newspaper. He leads class discussions about each piece, too. I'm nervous, knowing that he will call on me, knowing that he will advertise my article to everybody. Knowing that he might even ask me to recite it.

But I already know exactly what I want to say.

I have it all planned out in my mind.

Just like my plan for Ryan.

I met Ryan Thomas in the Gamer Club. Our club meets after school on Tuesdays in the computer lab, under the supervision of Mr. Li, the video production teacher. At our very first gathering, Mr. Li had us pull chairs away from the banks of computers to sit in a circle and introduce ourselves. He also asked us to list our favorite games or describe our favorite types of games.

"I'll go first!" Mr. Li said happily. "I love strategy games. Anything that requires me to think two steps ahead of my opponent."

My head spun with possible responses. But as each person shared, I started to wonder if I'd made a mistake joining this club. It seemed like everyone else was more serious about gaming than I was. In their introductions, the other kids boasted about their high scores and personal records, their amateur tournaments and league competition championships. Many used language and acronyms I'd never even heard of—FPS, MMO, RPG.

Meanwhile, the only real response I could think of was, *I like games because they're fun.*

Then Ryan's turn came: "Hey, I'm Ryan," he

said. He ruffled his blond hair as he spoke, running his fingers through the bangs that swooped across his forehead. "And I'll play anything, as long as it's fun; I'm just here for a good time. I like a lot of sports games—I play baseball and skateboard in real life. I also like stuff that scares me. That might sound weird, but whatever." He gave a rueful grin, and a few of us around the circle—myself included—smiled back at him, nodding. "Games with zombies, evil wizards, apocalypses, that sort of thing. Oh, and I love *Spacefaring Wanderers*. That one's my favorite right now."

Mr. Li thanked him for sharing, and my gaze lingered on Ryan. Golden-haired, green-eyed Ryan. It was still the beginning of the school year, and he looked like he'd spent the entire summer outdoors, his skin was so deeply bronzed, his suntan flaking around his elbows. His feet were fidgety beneath his chair; his fingers plucked at a beaded purple bracelet on his wrist.

Suddenly, it was my turn to speak. I cleared my throat and stared down at my hands, feeling uneasy with everyone's eyes on me.

"Hi, I'm Wesley," I said. "And I like games that are fun but challenging. My favorites usually have open, fantastical worlds. And side quests! I think I like doing the side quests even more than the main storyline sometimes, because they can be so quick and satisfying, and you tend to meet interesting characters or travel to cool corners of the map." I peeked around the circle, afraid that I was rambling too much, and Ryan caught my eye with an encouraging smile. I sat up a little straighter in my chair. "I also love a good puzzle or riddle. And for all those reasons combined, *Spacefaring Wanderers* is my favorite game ever."

There were a few appreciative nods around the group. Mr. Li enthusiastically thanked me for sharing. From his spot across the circle, Ryan gave me a discreet thumbs-up.

After that, I couldn't stop beaming.

3

Mom was late to pick me up that day. Almost everyone else from the Gamer Club had gone home, while I was still seated on the bench by the drop-off loop, waiting and watching each car that passed on the main street.

And Ryan was there, waiting for his ride, too.

I tried to distract myself. I don't have a cell phone—Mom is making me wait until I'm thirteen to get one—so I wasn't able to play games or text Hanan. Instead, I pulled my binder out of my backpack and flipped through my homework assignments.

As if I could concentrate on anything else.

As if I could ignore him as he drew closer, his fingers still plucking at his purple bracelet.

He met my gaze and asked, "Do you mind if I sit here?"

I scooted aside so fast, I nearly slid off the bench. He smiled as he sat down; I snapped my binder shut.

I was immediately struck by how good he smelled. Some boys my age drench themselves with gross and overwhelming colognes, but Ryan's scent was fresh and light and warm. Like laundry pulled straight from the dryer.

"Waiting for your parents?" he asked.

"My mom," I told him.

"Same. She said that she's running late because of Evil O."

I blinked. "She's, um—what?"

"Evil O." Ryan smirked and showed me his wrist. Just as I'd suspected, the bracelet looked like the product of a little kids' craft kit. The glossy purple strand was strung with colorful beads and five letter blocks, which spelled *EVILO*.

"My sister," Ryan explained. "She's seven and terrible and her name is Olive, but she put the letters on backward."

I laughed, surprised and delighted. "She must not be *that* terrible. It's a nice bracelet."

"Well, you weren't there when she raided my candy stash last Halloween."

"Ah." I shook my head in grave sympathy.

"Or the time she dropped my toy race car into our fish tank so the guppies wouldn't be bored."

"You're lucky," I told him. "I've always wanted siblings."

As soon as I spoke the words, Baby Zoe's sweet little face flashed in my mind. Her dark, twinkling eyes. Her drool-covered chin. She's technically my cousin: my mom's sister's daughter. But ever since Mom and I moved into Grandpa's house—along with my aunt and uncle and Zoe—it has felt like I gained a baby sister.

"Being an only child has its perks, though. I bet your house is so quiet. And you must have so much *space*. Your own room. Your own video game consoles. Your own everything."

I didn't want to correct him.

I didn't want to explain how I shared a bedroom with my mother. About the "rough patch" she was going through.

I didn't want to tell him about the complete lack of silence or space in Grandpa's house.

Instead, I said, "True. It isn't all bad."

Ryan's phone started ringing. He pulled it out of his pocket. Olive's number was saved in his contacts as *Lil Sis*, followed by a green olive emoji. The picture that filled his screen revealed a small blond girl, smiling crookedly at the camera, with wild swirls of pink and green marker ink drawn all over her face.

"Oh, look," Ryan said. "Chaos herself."

I giggled as he took the call. His mother had pulled into the wrong parking lot on campus, so Ryan spent the next few minutes attempting to redirect her through Olive, the seven-year-old copilot. Eventually, a midnight-blue SUV turned into the dropoff loop.

"There they are," he said, ending the call as Olive excitedly chanted: *I see you, I see you, I see you!* "Would you like a ride home?"

Warmth flooded my cheeks as I shook my head and said, "Oh, no. No. That's very kind of you, but my mom will be here any second."

"You sure? I promise, my mom won't mind."

The SUV pulled up to the curb. The back window rolled down, and Olive's skinny little arm stuck out as she waved frantically to her brother. "Ryan!" she shouted. "Ryan! Over here!"

He sighed. His voice turned solemn as he said, "The only problem is that you'll have to sit next to that little princess of terrors. And I can't be held accountable if she somehow manages to fling glitter all over you."

"She seems great, but I should wait for my mom. Thanks, though."

"Okay, then." Ryan stood up, hoisting his backpack straps higher onto his shoulders. "I'll see you around, Wesley."

"See you around," I echoed.

Ten minutes later, Mom's green Jeep came tearing into the drop-off loop. She plowed over the speed bumps, skidding to the yellow curb before me. As I climbed up into the passenger seat, she was breathlessly apologizing, explaining why she was late. And I only smiled and shrugged, content and adrift in my own thoughts about Ryan.

4

I finish my worksheet, and for the first time in weeks, all my homework assignments are done early. Even the stuff that is due Tuesday and Wednesday has been completed.

I sigh with relief. This feels like a good omen. And at last, the sun has risen, the world outside slowly brightening through shades of gray. Everything is shrouded in a fog so dense I can't even see the street beyond our front yard. Vader is still seated on the windowsill beside me. He watches the fog with narrowed green eyes, his ears angled forward, alert.

I've heard that fog banks like these are a sign that our ancestors are near. Perhaps this weather is a good omen, too.

I open my binder in my lap. Tuck this worksheet inside the interior flap, along with my other homework assignments and—the card.

The card that I made for Ryan.

The card that I plan to give him today.

I wriggle it free. Skim my fingertips across its surface. Pinch along its seam, straightening and deepening the fold.

When I made this card, I took a single sheet of plain white cardstock and folded it in half. Then I grabbed some colored pencils and a compass and a protractor to replicate the game map from *Spacefaring Wanderers* onto its front cover.

Spacefaring Wanderers is a video game set in an open galaxy. As your Wanderer avatar, you travel around in your spaceship to explore exciting, colorful planets. Each planet contains various quests to be completed, puzzles to be solved, and hidden gems to be collected. The quests and puzzles are how you earn points to level up; the gems are currency that allow you to customize your ship and your avatar's appearance.

There are also occasional battles with aliens. And rogue asteroids to avoid.

It's a lot of fun.

Recreating the map from the main menu was a long process, but only because I wanted it to look really good. I hope it will be a card worth keeping— something Ryan might want to hold on to. I drew clear, clean orbit rings with my compass. I colored the background in shades of violet and indigo to mimic the appearance of outer space. I took extra care to show the different textures of each planet on the map—some are freckled with craters, others have colorful swirls like marbles.

Then on the inside of the card, I wrote this simple poem:

Some planets are red
Some nebulas are blue
I could spend hours
Wandering the galaxy with you

Below this message, there is the word *Tolo?* written in careful block letters, followed by two options with checkboxes: *Yes* or *No*.

And I can only hope that he will check the *Yes*.

I pull my feet onto the couch, hugging my knees against my chest, the card pressed directly over my beating heart.

Vader reaches for me. He flexes his paw as he touches it to my shoulder, not scratching me, but seeking my attention. I turn to him, resting my cheek against the worn, lumpy couch cushion so that our noses nearly meet. His whiskers twitch. His green eyes are slits; he looks like he's on the cusp of a nap. His purrs reverberate in his throat.

"Don't worry," I tell him. "No matter what happens today, you're still my number one boy."

Vader squeezes his eyes shut and angles forward, crushing his cheek against my nose. I scratch him behind his ears as he drags his forehead back and forth, nuzzling me.

5

Mom is the first person to wake up. I hear the faint tones of our alarm going off in our room, and that's my cue to put the card away. I return it to my binder, which gets promptly zipped inside my backpack. Then I sprawl onto the couch, fluff the pillow behind my neck, and wait.

When Mom comes downstairs, she looks sleepy and disheveled—her eye mask pushed crookedly up onto her forehead, locks of hair slipping free from the braid that tumbles to her waist. She yawns and squints at me as she steps down from the staircase, dressed in baggy gray sweatpants and a faded black tank top.

My mother is beautiful. She is on the short side of average with lean, muscular arms and legs. Her hair is naturally dark brown, though she regularly dyes it to a burgundy shade similar to the color of cherry cola. Her skin is smooth and tan, with a smattering of brown freckles over her nose and temples. Her eyes are wide, and her irises are so dark they almost appear black, yet her gaze has this constant sparkle.

Vader—who loves my mother more than he loves me, unapologetically—immediately leaps from the windowsill and pounces across my belly, using me as a stepping stone to get to her faster. He meows and circles her feet, his tail curling around her calves as he presses against her legs, purring affectionately.

Mom's voice is groggy as she says, "Good morning. You're up early."

"Couldn't sleep."

"No? How come?"

I shrug. "Don't know. My homework is done, though. Can I watch TV before school?"

Mom yawns again. Rubs her eyes with the backs of her knuckles. "Sure. Just keep the volume down. What do you want for breakfast?"

"Whatever we have."

Mom nods and wanders into the kitchen, Vader trotting along at her heels.

I grab the remote and turn the TV on, navigating to my new favorite streaming app. Ryan actually introduced me to it—it's an app full of professional gamers, who share live feeds and recordings of themselves playing for fun and in tournaments. They are able to chat and interact with their fans, too.

I open the short list of channels I subscribe to; three gamers are online, including my favorite streamer, gemmakitty01, whose stream title makes me gasp:

Happy Indigenous Peoples' Day! | 24-Hour Live Charity Stream! | Come Watch Me Game and Chat with Native American Guest Stars!

Mom hears the gasp and pivots, glancing over her shoulder. "What happened?"

"Mom! Come here, come here, look!"

"Shhh."

I frantically whisper, "Come! *Look*."

Mom hurries back over, Vader scrambling to keep up.

Her mouth pops open as she reads the title. "Oh, wow. Is this Gemma?"

I click on the stream, and the screen fills up with an intense battle scene in the middle of an ancient-looking coliseum. The audio blasts in a rush of sword clangs. I flinch and squeeze the mute button, grimacing sheepishly.

Mom and I pause, waiting for Baby Zoe to wail, for the entire house to erupt. Vader tucks low and darts across the room to his scratching post, clobbering it with his claws, apparently inspired by the violence. But nothing else happens. The house remains still and silent.

"It's okay," Mom reassures me. "Grandpa and Kenji were watching the football game last night. They always forget to lower the volume before turning the TV off."

I breathe a sigh of relief. Then I lower the volume by several bars before unmuting.

Mom wrinkles her nose. "This isn't one of her normal games, right?"

I confirm, "It's not."

Normally, gemmakitty01 plays a lot of *Spacefaring Wanderers*, as well as other farming, puzzle, and simulation role-playing games. Her favorites have soothing soundtracks, pastel color palettes, and adorably animated characters.

This current game—which seems to be a gory battle royale, with gladiator avatars in a coliseum of sun-bleached stone and gritty sand—is unusual for her channel.

In the bottom corner of the screen, a small square shows a live feed of Gemma at her computer as she plays. Her hair is light pink and pulled back in a pair of pigtails; her cat-ear style headphones are also pink. Anime posters and floating bookshelves hover behind her, stacked with retro gaming consoles and cute stuffed animals.

In the top-middle part of the screen, there is a donation bar to log the amount of money her viewers have raised for charity. It's early in the day, so only a sliver of the bar is shaded in, but it's still cool to see.

Mom joins me on the couch. "Is Gemma Native?"

"I'm not sure. Maybe."

"Do you know where she's from? Where she lives?"

"Her profile just says central Oregon."

"Hmm. That could mean a lot of things. Maybe she's from Warm Springs?"

"Maybe."

Mom wraps her arms around me. She rests her cheek against my hair. As I lean into her embrace, Vader hops onto the couch and curls up in Mom's lap.

6

For a long time, it was just the three of us: Mom, Vader, and me.

We lived in a cozy little apartment in Lynnwood, Washington, just outside of Seattle. We had a balcony with a view of the I-5 corridor, plus the wide bank of evergreen trees beyond the freeway's concrete walls. At night, we'd sit out there with mugs of hot cocoa, watching the cars roar down the gray-striped lanes, the way that I imagine people in the countryside might stare at the stars.

The apartment complex also had a swimming pool. Each summer, my friends would come over and we'd spend hours splashing around in its turquoise water before gathering in the living room to stream movies and TV shows. The entire apartment would smell like chlorine and popcorn, which are pretty much the two greatest scents in the world. Then Vader would inevitably squat in his litter box, which led to the *worst* scent in the world.

Life was good. We were happy.

And Mom and I have always been so close. I'm *always* proud to call her my mom. But I notice the way other adults glance at her sometimes, their gazes cutting and judgmental. I've heard their rude assumptions when they speak to her.

Sometimes people are mean.

A few years ago, Mom took me to the Emerald City Comic Con for my eighth birthday. It was the best gift ever, and she made it even better by designing costumes for us to dress up as Gamora and Baby Groot from *Guardians of the Galaxy*. We spent the whole day laughing and making space puns and wandering around the exhibition halls. We marveled at limited edition figurines and geeky art prints and displays of rare, pristine comic books sheathed in plastic wrap. We received a ton of compliments on our costumes and took a million photos.

It was almost a perfect day.

Then this one lady asked for permission to take a picture with us. We happily agreed and posed alongside her, and it was nice, until the woman patted Mom's arm and said, "Thanks, hon. It's so sweet of you to dress up with your little sister like this."

Mom gave a lighthearted laugh and said, "She's actually my daughter. But thanks."

The woman glanced between us, owl-eyed. "Your daughter?"

"Yep!" Mom said. "That's why she's my Baby Groot. Not my Nebula."

The woman continued to stare.

"I was really young when I had her," Mom explained with a shrug. "It hasn't always been easy, but I wouldn't change a thing. She's the brightest star in my sky."

Mom beamed and reached for me, but I shrank back from her, feeling embarrassed. I didn't understand why she was still talking to this stranger. I didn't like how that one sentence started: *It hasn't always been easy.*

The woman responded, "So I suppose there isn't a Star-Lord in the picture, then?" And the tone of her words made me feel even worse.

Mom flinched. Between my rejected touch and the woman's sudden coldness, she was momentarily stunned.

Then, softly, she said, "Wesley, let's get going."

I followed her out of the exhibition hall, down the miles-long escalators, through the crowded ground floor of the convention center, and out to the row of food trucks lined up along the sidewalk. We ordered gyros and Greek fries and ate quietly, side by side. It was an overcast afternoon in March, the air cool and carrying the smell of rain, even as buttery sunshine spilled through gaps in the graphite clouds.

I felt guilty for pulling away, for getting upset over my mom's words. I felt angry with that woman, whose rudeness had tainted a happy moment. I didn't understand why strangers felt an urge to put my mother down, just because she was young and had chosen to raise me on her own. But I also didn't understand why my mother willingly said things like: *It hasn't always been easy, but . . .*

I overheard those same words three years later, while Mom was on the phone with our landlord. She was asking him for an extension on the rent. Her voice was soft and pleading.

"Business has been slow this month," she said. "They raised the rent on my chair at the salon again . . . Yes, I understand . . . I know, I know . . . It hasn't always been easy, but . . . Okay. I'll figure something else out."

That "something else" turned out to be our living arrangements. Mom could no longer afford to keep us in the apartment.

So that night, Mom made two steaming mugs of hot cocoa and took me out to the balcony to break the news as gently as she could. She explained her plan for us to move into Grandpa's house. We would stay with him and Auntie Jess and Uncle Kenji for a while.

"The baby will be here in a few weeks," Mom said. "Won't that be fun? You've always wanted a little sister. Now you'll be able to see your new cousin and snuggle with her and play with her whenever you want."

I nodded, wanting to be brave and cooperative for Mom, even though I was also a little skeptical. I loved my family, and I was excited to meet the baby—but Grandpa's house wasn't very big. It was a two-story house with a small square footprint, three tiny bedrooms, and one-point-five bathrooms. Would Mom and I be able to fit two beds and all our clothes into her childhood room? Would the baby cry a lot at night? Would I ever be able to invite my friends over?

I asked Mom, "Will we ever come back to our apartment?"

Mom tried to smile. She said, "It's possible."

My heart sank. Because whenever Mom says *It's possible*, she usually means *No*.

7

As we continue to watch gemmakitty01's livestream, Mom and I learn that there is a long list of Native American guest stars who will take turns gaming with her today. Among them are artists and activists and academics, comic book writers and musicians and voice actors. The twenty-four-hour livestream is divided into forty-five-minute gaming sessions and fifteen-minute intermissions. Gemma posted the full schedule of guests and games across her social media platforms.

We also learn that the money raised during this

charity stream will all go to Native American child welfare programs.

Eventually, Mom squeezes my shoulder and returns to the kitchen to make breakfast. Vader also rises, stretching himself tall, arching his back into an upside-down U. He yawns wide, showing his pointy teeth, his scaly pink tongue. Then he leaps to the floor and saunters over to his scratching post, digging his claws into its frayed, carpeted ledge.

Grandpa and Uncle Kenji are the next two people to awaken and come downstairs. They each greet me and Mom, and fill up mugs with black coffee, before wandering over to join me in the living room.

"You know, back in my day," Uncle Kenji says, with a sidelong glance at the television, "we actually played our video games. We didn't sit around watching other people like this."

"Back in my day," Grandpa counters, as he settles onto the couch beside me, "we only played them at the arcade! Which is how it should be. These young people today, with all their options, all their *devices*."

"It's not healthy," Uncle Kenji agrees.

"It's not normal," Grandpa says meaningfully.

Thankfully, the gladiator gaming session that we first tuned in to has ended. At the moment, gemmakitty01 is playing a racing game with a group of Native comedians who are all talking fast and making jokes as they crash into the walls and each other.

"Do you think she knows that other colors exist?" Grandpa asks.

Uncle Kenji says, "She *is* surrounded by pink, isn't she?"

"I think Gemma's cute," Mom says, as she exits the kitchen with two full plates of food. "With her pink kitty headphones, and her pink hair, and her pink keyboard."

"It's a bit much," Grandpa grumps. "Variety is good, you know. For the soul."

Mom rolls her eyes. "It's her stream and her stuff, Dad. She's allowed to do whatever she wants. Wesley, come help me clear the table so we can eat. Dad, Kenji, there are more eggs and such for everyone—feel free to help yourselves."

I jump up and cross the room. The dining table is constantly cluttered in this house. Things have a way of piling up there: junk mail, my schoolwork, Baby Zoe's teething toys. I help Mom shove everything into a pile in the far corner, away from our two seats. Then I sit in my wicker chair, while she sets the plates down and hurries back into the kitchen to grab more stuff.

Grandpa says, "And I still don't understand how this streaming business works, if I'm being honest."

Uncle Kenji slurps his coffee and nods.

"I mean, this is supposedly her full-time job? This is what she does? She plays video games. All day long."

"That's right," Mom says, as she returns with a carton of orange juice tucked under her arm and two glasses pinched between her fingertips. "She gets sponsorships and paid advertisers on her channel."

"And tips and subscriptions," I add helpfully.

"Doesn't she also have her own merchandise?" Mom asks. "An online shop?"

I say, "She does! She sells a bunch of different T-shirts and hats and stuff, plus she has her own special edition controllers and headphones."

"I wonder if they all have the kitty ears," Uncle Kenji muses.

I tell him, "I don't know. Probably."

Mom hands me a full glass of orange juice, and I take a moment to thank her for breakfast. She made sunny-yellow scrambled eggs, served with clusters of green grapes and perfectly browned, buttered toast.

Grandpa continues to squint at the television screen. He looks like he's attempting to watch a foreign language film with microscopic subtitles. After a long pause, he declares: "I don't get it."

"What don't you get, Dad?" Mom asks.

"How is this a real job? She's not working; she's sitting around on the computer! And what's the point of it? Watching someone else's game, instead of playing it yourself?"

"Isn't that exactly what Grandpa and Uncle Kenji do when they watch football?" I whisper to Mom. She guffaws in response, nearly choking on her first sip of orange juice.

"*What* did Wesley just say?" Grandpa shouts.

"Nothing," Mom singsongs, shooting me a wink.

Uncle Kenji, on the other hand, stares at me with a wide-eyed, gobsmacked look of betrayal. He releases a long, low whistle and says, "Oof."

Grandpa crosses his arms over his chest. "This racing game defies physics," he mutters, unable to take his eyes off the screen.

_8_

Here are a few things to know about my family:

Grandpa Mac Wilder is the Elder, the patriarch, the original owner of the house we all live in. He used to work as a mail carrier for the US Postal Service, but he had to stop after he injured his shoulder playing basketball. He was out of work for a long time after that, which is why my Auntie Jess and Uncle Kenji moved back in with him—to help him out with cooking and cleaning while he recovered, and also to help him pay the bills. These days, Grandpa is a substitute bus driver for the school district. He also babysits Baby Zoe on his days off. Grandpa has a big, loud laugh. He loves to go hiking, fishing, and camping. And scary movies are his favorite movies. For some weird reason.

Grandpa's daughters are my mom and Auntie Jess. He was married to my grandmother, Denise, for over twenty years; she died when I was a toddler, so I don't have many of my own memories with her. But I love it when Grandpa shares his. He tells stories about her baking, singing along to the radio, and voting and canvassing in every single election.

Mom and Auntie Jess join in, too. They'll recall Grandma Denise taking them with her to stand in long lines for the sake of American democracy. They remember her lectures about the importance of showing up and giving back to their communities, which is one reason why Mom and Auntie Jess always vote in tribal elections, too. On rainy Saturday mornings, Mom and Jess will also take turns cracking eggs, measuring spoonfuls of sugar, kneading dough, and squinting at the smudged cursive instructions on Grandma Denise's yellowed recipe cards. Whenever their bakes come out of the oven, I always tell them things like *These are the best chocolate chip cookies I've ever tasted*, or *Can you make me this cake for my next birthday party?*

And they'll be happy and grateful for the praise. But almost every time, the two sisters will smile and shrug and say, *It's pretty good. But it's not as good as Mom's.*

It's always a bit sad. But also very sweet.

Auntie Jess is my mom's little sister. She's an emergency room nurse, so she works long, hard hours, and she consumes a ton of energy drinks. There is an entire shelf in our fridge filled with tall, skinny, rainbow-colored cans that no one else is allowed to touch. Especially not me, since I am twelve. But personally, I'm not interested in them anyway. Jess is also the best gift-giver in the entire family; she always brings piles of presents to my birthday parties. Plus, she loves show tunes and nail polish and chocolate just as much as I do.

Uncle Kenji is married to Auntie Jess. Kenji is a science teacher. He works at a middle school in Mukilteo, where he organizes student ski trips in the winters, and coaches track and field athletes in the springtime. Kenji also took me and Hanan on a trip to the mountains once, and he attempted to teach us both how to snowboard—we weren't very good at it, but we had fun regardless.

Baby Zoe is Jess and Kenji's daughter. She is eight months old. She's plump and sweet, with feathery black hair and bright brown eyes. I'm pretty much convinced that she is the cutest baby in the world.

My mother's name is Cadence. She is a cosmetologist, a cosplayer, and a really great mom. She is creative and kind and generous. Bighearted and open-minded. She makes time for everyone, and she is willing to befriend almost anyone. She loves people.

With one notable exception.

My father.

We don't live with him. We don't interact with him. And we don't really talk about him.

The last time I saw him, I was ten years old; it did not end well.

9

Time for school.

I have a queasy feeling in my stomach, as I trudge up the stairs to change into my clothes and brush my hair and teeth before I leave to catch the bus. I can't stop thinking about my poem, printed in the school newspaper. About the card tucked inside my binder. About everything that might or might not happen today.

I've never been to a school dance before, but that's what the Tolo is—a school dance. This is my first year in middle school, my first year where Tolos and other dances are even an option for students. (The square-dancing unit in our sixth-grade PE curriculum clearly doesn't count.)

At my school, it's traditional for girls to ask boys to be their dates for Tolos, instead of the other way around. I don't know why we need a special kind of event for girls to ask boys, or why it's called a "Tolo," but whatever. That's not the point.

The point is: I'm nervous. And excited. And uncertain. And giddy. And scared. And hopeful.

Here is how I'm going to do it: Ryan always goes to the computer lab during lunch. He and his friends gather there to play *Spacefaring Wanderers* under Mr. Li's supervision.

He will be seated at Computer #7, because that's his favorite monitor, the one he always chooses.

I will tap him on the shoulder. He will turn to face me, and I'll hold up my copy of the school newspaper to tell him, "Ryan, did you see that you were mentioned in the paper today?"

This will surprise him. He won't actually be featured in the paper at all. (Hanan assured me of that.) But he will ask me to show him, and I will tell him to turn to page seven. (Seven is his lucky number, I think; it's also the number on his baseball jersey.) And right there, taped to the top of the page, he will find the card that I made for him. He will see the illustration of the solar system from our favorite game. He will see the poem that I wrote for him. He will see the two checkboxes: *Yes* or *No*.

I have my plan. The card is finished and ready to go. The newspapers will be printed and waiting in Ms. Roux's classroom. All I have to do is make it through the bus ride, my morning classes, and the beginning of my lunch period—then I will go to him, and ask him to the Tolo, and I can finally stop fretting over it.

Easy peasy.

10

Auntie Jess and Baby Zoe are downstairs when I return. They are both seated on a soft pink blanket, surrounded by alphabet blocks and rattle toys. Auntie Jess is slouching and massaging her temples; she is wearing her favorite pink silk nightgown with big, metallic peonies all over it, and her nails are painted in a glossy French manicure. Zoe is happily knocking two of her blocks together, giggling as drool streams down her chin; a cloth bib is pinned around her neck, and her footed onesie is patterned with little yellow ducks.

Grandpa is still on the couch, watching gemma-kitty01's livestream with the volume turned way down. She and her guests are playing another game now, one that appears to be set in a mystical forest. Mom is washing the dishes in the kitchen. I'm not sure where Uncle Kenji is.

When Baby Zoe hears me coming, she turns and gasps and smiles. Her bright brown eyes shine as she reaches for me with both of her chubby little arms.

I drop to my knees on the blanket. "Good morning, Auntie. Good morning, Zoe." I give Zoe a big hug, pressing my cheek against hers; her skin is smooth and warm, and she smells like baby lotion. I squeeze her and rock her back and forth in my lap.

"Good morning, Wes," Auntie Jess says, yawning. "Excited for school today?"

"Kind of?"

"So what's up with this Gemma, anyway?" Grandpa asks me. "Are she and her friends Native? Before your aunt and cousin came down, they were talking about Indigenous Peoples' Day."

I perk up. "I don't know if Gemma is, but her guests definitely are. She's doing a twenty-four-hour charity stream for the holiday today."

"Really?" Jess looks surprised. "How cool."

Grandpa nods his approval. "Yeah. That is pretty cool, actually." And I must be smiling too big or something, because he suddenly frowns and adds: "I still don't see how this counts as real work, though."

"For some people, creating online content is a full-time job," Auntie Jess says.

"For some people, clocking in from nine-to-five for an actual employer is what real, *honest* work is all about." He waves one hand at the screen. "These kids are just off having fun. Playing around in fantasy worlds."

Auntie Jess shrugs. "If people can survive by doing what they love, let them. What's the harm?"

"Oh, *sheesh*," Grandpa says, as he refocuses on the TV screen. He leans forward, placing his elbows on his knees. He gives an ominous chuckle. "Well, guess I can't argue with that, Jess. But there might be some harm in *this*, hmm?"

Jess and I look up at the TV. Onscreen, Gemma and her guests appear to be in a boss battle against a purple owl with huge yellow eyes and talons. Even with the volume turned down, I can hear the gamers shrieking as they attempt to defeat it.

Jess grimaces. "Oh, geez. Hopefully none of the guests are very religious?"

Grandpa keeps on chuckling. "It's only a game, to be fair."

"I know. But still. Some folks take the owl thing pretty seriously."

"What 'owl thing'?" I ask them.

Grandpa meets my gaze. "Lots of Natives get severely creeped out by owls," he explains. "Some religiously traditional people associate them with death and evil spirits. And in the old days, when many tribes lived closer to nature, parents warned their kids to stay quiet during the night, or else an owl might *swoop* silently into their camps and SNATCH the children away with their *sharp, gigantic TALONS!*" Grandpa snarls and swats menacingly at the air, his hand curled like a claw.

Auntie Jess sighs and massages her temples again. Baby Zoe laughs and throws her blocks and starts to clap for Grandpa.

A chill rolls down my spine as I ask, "Well. What do we believe?"

"We?" Grandpa smirks. "You get to decide for yourself, Wesley. You have your own free mind."

I try again: "But what do *you* believe?"

Grandpa shrugs. Leans back against the couch. "To me, an owl is just a bird who happens to fly around at night."

I slouch a little bit, mirroring Auntie Jess.

Mom clears her throat behind me. "Wesley, you better get moving before you miss the bus."

"Okay," I say, as I get to my feet.

Auntie Jess turns to Mom. "Hey, Cadence, can I borrow your camera?"

"What for?" Mom asks.

"Zoe's eight months old today; it's time for her next photo shoot."

"Okay. Just make sure you put it on the charger when you're done. I want to have enough battery for the powwow at Coastline tonight."

I shove my feet into my shoes. Hoist my backpack straps onto my shoulders. Pick up my viola case. My stomach feels all funny and queasy again, because this is it—I'm going to school. I'm going to ask Ryan to be my date to the Tolo. I'm going to see my poem in the newspaper.

It's all going to happen so very soon.

I wave and say goodbye to everyone in the room. Then, as I start to leave . . .

"Wesley?"

I pause with my hand on the doorknob. "Yeah, Mom?"

"Good luck with everything today," she says with a smile and a wink. There's a sly note in her voice that makes my cheeks go warm, makes me wonder if she is capable of reading my mind. If she could somehow know about the secret thoughts in my head. The card in my binder. The tenderness in my heart.

But that doesn't seem likely.

I must be imagining things.

Or at least that's what I tell myself, as I turn from her glimmering brown gaze and walk out the door.

11

It's a foggy morning. The gray mist is so thick in the air, it seems as if the two-story roofs and treetops around me have been rubbed out with an eraser. As if the entire neighborhood has been swallowed by clouds. The road at my feet is a dark stripe across the ground, leading farther into the depths of the grayness, dissolving from sight. My hand aches with the weight of my viola case; my backpack straps dig into my shoulders. And every sound—from my footsteps to the car idling in my neighbor's driveway to the rasp of a crimson leaf hitting the pavement—seems too quiet in the muffled stillness of the fog.

It's somehow eerie and peaceful at the same time. October at its finest.

As I walk along, I keep thinking about owls, wondering about the stories and tribes that Grandpa spoke of. Owls have never scared me before; I mostly associate them with knowledge and wisdom, probably because of the owl characters and mascots I've seen in school. They also make me think of babies and little kids, because back when Mom and I went shopping for Auntie Jess's baby shower, owls were *everywhere* in the stores' baby departments: patterned on blankets and onesies and hooded towels.

I find stuff like this fascinating. Humans are all so different in the way they view things. One person might love owls and think they're cute and smart. Someone else might be deathly afraid of them. The same can be true for spiders, or dogs, or raccoons.

A sudden scuffling from somewhere nearby makes me flinch hard, stopping me at the edge of the road. I stand and stare through the fog. I'm right where our cul-de-sac ends and the woods begin. When the neighbors put their house on the market last year, the real estate flyers excitedly advertised the "greenbelt" that surrounded our neighborhood, offering "privacy and serenity" to the local residents. Mom and I used to visit Grandpa and go hunting for fairies in this small patch of forest, back when I was really little and believed in such things.

I'm not sure what I believe now. But I know I heard something. Movement.

The woods are shrouded in fog. I can only see the closest branches; some are drooping and heavy with dark-green needles; others are angular and golden leafed and lichen spotted. Their knobby trunks are marked with tufts of soft, seafoam-green bristles.

From somewhere in the depths of the mist, I hear it again. Rustling.

Then a squirrel darts out from beneath a fern, zigzagging wildly across the street, his gray-brown tail bobbing as he goes. His abrupt appearance makes me gasp and stumble, though I immediately feel silly as I watch him scamper up the length of a telephone pole.

I take a deep breath. Readjust my grip on the viola case. How embarrassing. At least no one was here to witness my fear over a squirrel.

Moving along.

I hurry across the street and around the corner, following the sidewalk that pops up on this length of the road. I keep a brisk pace, because the bus will be here soon. I keep my gaze down, focused.

Too late, I start to second-guess my outfit for the day. My white sneakers are scuffed and worn; they have brownish laces and are marked with grass-stain smears. Normally, I don't mind wearing these shoes; they're not pretty to look at, but they are comfortable and suitable for long days out. My only other options include: a pair of rain boots that pinch my pinkie toes, a sturdy set of hiking boots that would look odd at school, some seasonally impractical sandals, and a delicate pair of pastel-purple ballet flats. The flats are pristine and topped with a little golden bow. I never wear them to school. They're too nice, and I would hate for them to get ruined somehow.

But should I have made an exception? Today feels special. Significant. Will Ryan be impressed when I approach him in the same old tattered sneakers that I wear 99 percent of the time at school?

And what about the rest of my outfit? Blue jeans. A commemorative Emerald City Comic Con shirt of heathered blue cotton, with lime-green lettering. A plain, purple zip-up hoodie. The same hoodie that I wear about 50 percent of the time. Almost every other day.

My stomach lurches. I feel suddenly insecure in my own ordinariness.

But it's too late to turn back now.

12

I hear the kids gathered at my bus stop before I see them. Their voices rise like the crest of an approaching wave. The fog starts to dissolve around them as I draw closer to the intersection.

Most of them are eighth graders that I don't know well and never talk to, so I hover at the edge of their circle. I set my viola case on the ground beside my feet and flex my fingers. Shake out the sore muscles in my hand.

"Hey! Hey, you, girl."

It takes me a moment to realize that one of the

eighth graders, a boy named Brady, is speaking to me.

"Yes, *you*," he shouts at me. "Bandits or Raiders?"

His friends are all snickering and watching me. Like they're sharing an inside joke. And the joke is me.

Randomly receiving their attention is bewildering. It robs me of my entire vocabulary.

"I'm s-sorry, what?"

"Bandits or Raiders," he says again, sounding exasperated. "I'm asking you to settle an argument for me."

"Dude," his friend says. "You can't get some random girl's opinion. It doesn't count."

"She doesn't even know what you're talking about," another one adds.

"Okay, but the Bandits—"

I am immediately forgotten. Their conversation continues; their circle closes. They move on and I am left standing here, feeling embarrassed, turning his words over in my mind until it clicks.

Bandits vs. Raiders. It's a video game. The goal of the gameplay is to capture the enemy team's flag and defend your team's territory across various maps. The players are all divided into two camps: Bandits or Raiders.

He was asking me to pick a side.

I spend the next few minutes reimagining our encounter. I picture myself standing tall and telling Brady: *It makes no difference. Their power-ups are all the same and the maps are mirror images of each other, so it doesn't matter whether you're a Bandit or a Raider.* I debate whether or not I should interrupt them and make it clear that I actually do know what he was talking about, that I've played the game before, and that my opinion counts. Because it does.

But then the bus arrives.

And the moment passes.

Which is fine. I have nothing to prove to them, anyway.

(Right?)

As soon as I board the bus, my best friend, Hanan, pops up in our seat and motions for me to come quickly, her hazel eyes wide to convey urgency.

I move down the aisle with my viola case held awkwardly in front of me, hugged against my chest. I try to avoid bumping into backpacks and brown vinyl seats. I try to ignore another burst of shouts and snickering from the eighth-grade boys as they settle into the coveted back rows of the bus.

By the time I reach Hanan, she practically lunges for me.

"Have you seen it?" she demands. "Has anyone shown you yet?"

"Can I sit, please?"

She scoots over, pressing her back against the smeary windowpane. "For the record," she says, "I would have told you last night, but my mom wouldn't let me log on to *Spacefaring Wanderers*. We had more of her 'screen-free family fun.'" She rolls her eyes. "She's still trying to get me into that card game."

Hanan's mom did the same thing at our last sleepover. She made us stop in the middle of a complicated side quest in *Spacefaring Wanderers* so she could teach us how to play rummy. We sat at the dining table with her, and she brought out a pot of tea steeped with fresh mint leaves and did her best to persuade us that her game was a million times better than ours. *Come on, girls*, she said in her Syrian accent. *This is the real fun. Sitting together, talking, no screens in front of your faces. Much, much better. Million times.*

I smirk. "Did she let you win at all?"

"Of course not," Hanan says bitterly. "She sucks at explaining the rules, and there's some secret strategy that she wants me to magically figure out on my own. *Just use your brain, it's not that hard*, she tells me. And she seriously wonders why I never want to play with her!"

I can't help but chuckle.

"But that is not the point right now," Hanan says, narrowing her eyes at me. "The PTP account. Have you seen it?"

"What? I have no idea what you're talking about."

She grimaces. "Oh no. That's what I was afraid of." Hanan pulls her phone out and holds it up for me to see, as she opens her folder of social media apps. "I'm really sorry, Wesley," she says. "But this involves Ryan."

13

My blood runs cold. "What do you mean?"

Hanan squints at her screen, typing frantically into a search bar. "Hold on, just give me a second—"

"What do you mean?" I repeat, the panic creeping into my voice.

"This," Hanan says, thrusting her phone into my face. "This, right here."

I stare at the profile she has opened. I see a grid of colored squares, each lined with neat rows of text. They alternate between purple backgrounds with gold letters and gold backgrounds with purple letters—our school colors. I click on a square to enlarge it; the text says: *Saylor May Rasmussen & Liam Winkler.*

Saylor May and Liam are both seventh graders. Saylor May is in my English and PE classes; Liam went to my elementary school.

"Someone made this account last night," Hanan explains. "PTP stands for Panthers Tolo Predictions. And they posted this . . ." Hanan reaches over to zoom back out and scroll down. She clicks on a square toward the bottom of the page.

Ella Holland & Ryan Thomas.

Oh.

Ella.

Ella and Ryan.

I feel suddenly nauseated as I ask, "Is this real? Are they going to Tolo?"

"No," Hanan says. "Or at least, I don't think so. These are all *predictions*." She bites her bottom lip. "But it could happen."

Ella Holland. She is one of the richest, blondest girls in our school. She is pretty and popular and (possibly?) nice, although I kind of think she seems like a snob. Because she gets dropped off at school in her mom's glossy red sports car every morning. She has a designer backpack patterned with a rainbow of some brand's repeating logo. And there's just something about the lift of her chin when she walks down the halls, the constant, straight-faced coolness in her gaze.

I don't think I've ever heard her laugh.

I'm not even sure if I've seen her smile.

Hanan must be capable of reading my mind, because she shoots me a look. "Girl, Ella Holland has never done or said anything mean to you. You have no reason to hate her."

"I don't hate her," I say with a flinch.

"Your face says otherwise."

"I don't even know her. But I don't hate anyone. Hate is an ugly word."

That's a lesson that has been drilled into me by my mother. *Hate is an ugly word*, she would say to me, back when I was small and prone to tantrums. *We do not hate things in this house.*

"You dislike her then," Hanan corrects.

"I don't," I say.

I refocus on the phone, scrolling down slightly to view the likes and comments. There are dozens of heart-shaped reactions, and way more remarks from people than I expected. There are more than fifty comments. The top two make my stomach curl. The first is from Dante Rawlins, Ryan's best friend: a wide-eyed emoji, followed by a smirk emoji; the second is from Saylor May Rasmussen, who wrote: *haha aww both blondies!*

I cross my arms and look away. "These predictions don't mean anything. We don't even know if Ella *likes* Ryan."

"She might not," Hanan allows. "But they're both—you know, North Shore kids."

North Shore kids is a term for the popular, overachiever crowd in our school. Because most of them happen to come from the wealthiest part of our district's neighborhood. The ones who board buses bound for the mansions down by the North Shore waterfront.

Hanan and I are not on one of those buses.

I say, "That doesn't automatically mean they like each other, or that they even know each other."

"True. I'm just saying that group tends to stick together."

I'm not sure how to respond to that; she's not wrong.

"For what it's worth, I'm still rooting for you," Hanan declares, as she drops her phone back into her backpack. "And sure, being a North Shore kid isn't everything. You and Ryan are in the Gamer Club together. Maybe you two will have more in common than him and Ella."

I search Hanan's face. Her eyeliner is winged today, the dark tips emphasizing the green-gold flecks in her hazel eyes. She normally straightens her light-brown hair, but this morning, her natural curls are held back by a blue headband.

"Hanan?"

"Hmm?"

"Were we mentioned at all?"

She gives me a blank look. "Were we mentioned where?"

"On that account. The Tolo predictions."

Her eyes spark with something like surprise. Then she blinks and shakes her head and says, "Uh, no. No."

"Do you have any idea who created it?"

"Nah," she says. "It was all totally anonymous. But I think it was one of the North Shore seventh graders. Almost all of the pairings were among them."

_14_

Shorelands Middle School. Home of the Panthers.

Our school is located at the bottom of a hill. Wide, spotless sidewalks and neatly trimmed hedges wrap around its perimeter. Buses inch through the morning traffic like a group of giant yellow caterpillars. I watch out the window as we pass by the kids bicycling and walking to school, and all the gridlocked cars in the main parking lot, their brake lights glowing red through the thinning fog.

I glimpse a midnight-blue SUV in the crowd and crane my neck, curious to see if the car belongs to

Ryan's mom. Sometimes I wonder if I made the right choice, turning down a ride from him that day.

Hanan elbows me hard in the ribs. "Hello?" she snaps. "Are you even listening to me?"

"Sorry," I say, cringing as I shift my attention back to her. "What's up?"

She huffs. "I was *asking* if you're coming with me to Ms. Roux's class."

"Oh, yeah. Definitely."

Today's finished copies of the *Shorelands Times* will be in her classroom; Hanan always goes there early on Monday mornings, to help distribute them across the campus.

I think of the card in my binder. The first step of my grand gesture for Ryan is finished; the second step is to grab a copy of the paper. Then all I have to do is find him in the computer lab during lunch. That's step three.

I take a deep breath. One step at a time today. One step at a time.

As we approach the bus loop, I reposition my viola case in my lap. Its worn leather is covered in colorful stickers: a pink doughnut with rainbow sprinkles, the blue NASA logo, an animated gemma-kitty01 avatar, and other various designs with looping cursive texts and watercolor details.

Ryan complimented them once. It was the second week of school, and we crossed paths in the hallway. He smiled at me and said, "Hey, Wesley! Nice stickers. I didn't know you play the violin."

I was so flattered and flustered by him, I only waved in response. I didn't even correct his assumption about which instrument I play. And I didn't think fast enough to say thank you, or to compliment him back.

The bus whines to a stop. I hug my viola case to my chest as I stand up.

Hanan and I follow the stream of people exiting the bus, then we hurry across the blacktop and cut through the middle of the campus. We drop my viola off in the music room and keep going. Ms. Roux's classroom is in one of the portables by the gym, across from the track and field, near the edge of the school's property.

We hurry up the ramp that leads to P3-2. A laminated poster outlines Ms. Roux's class expectations: *Be kind to others; Be responsible for your actions; Keep your phone and personal electronics put away.*

I follow Hanan inside. The desks are arranged in cramped groups of four. There is a small bookcase in the corner, stuffed with worn, creased paperbacks. The American flag is hung above Ms. Roux's desk, which is piled high with stacks of today's newspaper.

Ms. Roux peeks at us from behind one stack. "Oh, good!" she exclaims. "Hanan, I'm so glad you brought Wesley with you today."

Ms. Roux pushes her chair back and rounds the desk to greet us. She's short enough to be mistaken for a student from behind. She has big blue eyes, magnified by thick-rimmed glasses; her wildly curly, strawberry-blond hair is styled in a bun that is straining to break free from its bobby pins. Her dark blue dress is patterned with yellow pencils.

"Wesley," she says. "I just loved your piece in the paper. Very, very well written."

I can't help but blush. "Thank you."

"You should submit to us more often. You know we love to prioritize diverse voices and perspectives in the *Shorelands Times*! Isn't that right, Hanan?"

Hanan gives her a hand salute.

"Can I see it? My piece?" I ask sheepishly.

Ms. Roux whisks a copy from the top of the nearest stack and passes it to me with a flourish.

Hanan inches closer, peering over my shoulder as I flip through it, the nerves coiling in my stomach. The pages smell of fresh ink. They're still warm from the printer.

There I am.

"We Still Belong: An Indigenous Peoples' Day Poem! by Wesley Wilder, Grade 7" appears at the top of the column. The verses that I wrote are printed beneath it in neat, tiny stanzas.

All my thoughts about this holiday. All my positive feelings about my Native ancestry and identity. All my hard work, multiple drafts and revisions, and changes throughout the process of editing.

Hanan grins and nudges me. "That's all you," she says.

I smile back.

All me.

15

There aren't many Native kids at my school. Less than 2 percent of our student population is listed as Native. And sometimes I wonder if I even count as one.

Grandpa, Auntie Jess, and Mom are all members of the Upper Skagit Indian Tribe. Upper Skagit is a federally recognized tribe with a reservation community in northwestern Washington State. Grandpa's grandparents were born there. Grandpa's father was, too, but he left home to attend the University of Washington in Seattle, where he became a mechanical engineer. He then worked for the Boeing Company and raised his family in Everett, Washington. Grandpa was close with his parents and eventually bought his own house in Everett to stay near them. He raised Mom and Jess there, and we all continue to live there now.

My great-great-grandmother was an Upper Skagit woman; Lushootseed was her first language, before she was sent to boarding schools where all the Native kids were required to speak English. Her husband was also Native, but for some reason, he rejected registering with any particular tribe. Grandpa says his refusal was a political statement, but I'm not really sure how or why he did it. Their son, my great-grandfather, married a white woman, the daughter of Dutch immigrants and tulip farmers. My grandpa also married a non-Native woman, Grandma Denise. And my biological father is white.

There are over one thousand different tribes across North America; each one has its own enrollment rules and tribal laws, but many tribes determine their citizenship in the same way: blood quantum laws. The Upper Skagit Indian Tribe uses blood quantum for enrollment. And since I am technically "one-sixteenth" Upper Skagit, my blood quantum is too low to gain citizenship status. Mom and Auntie Jess were the end of the line in our family; unless the laws change, Baby Zoe and I will never be Upper Skagit "enough" to become members of the tribe. This means that we will never get to vote in tribal elections or gain other treaty rights that our ancestors fought for. Like hunting and fishing around the Skagit River.

It's weird for me. I don't really care about the hunting and fishing stuff, because guns scare me and the idea of hunting anything makes me squeamish. But no matter what, I wish I could become a tribal member. I wish I could be included. I wish I felt like I could belong there.

Mom and Grandpa and Auntie all insist that the blood quantum stuff doesn't matter. They say that in our family, we are all equal and important and Native.

But I think I will always feel a little different. And there's nothing I can do about it.

I'm still proud of my heritage. I try to be a part of the local Native community as much as I can.

That's one reason why I wrote a column for the school newspaper today.

It's also why I tried to join the Native/Indigenous Student Union.

_16_

During the first week of school, there was a club fair in the cafeteria. A bunch of different groups set up trifolds on the long tables, along with props and flyers and printed photographs to attract new members. That was how I found the Gamer Club. Mr. Li and the club's eighth-grade leaders had a collection of Game Boy Colors on display, which Hanan thought were vintage and nerdy, but I was ecstatic. I thought they were amazing.

After I signed up for the Gamer Club, Hanan and I continued to make our way around the fair. We'd wanted to join a club together, but we quickly learned that—despite being best friends—we had wildly different tastes in after-school activities. (Which is my polite way of saying that Hanan can be super picky.)

When I asked about the Cheer Squad, Hanan scoffed and said, "Let's just wait until high school. That's when the cheerleaders actually get to compete and do cool stuff."

When we stopped by the Cooking Club's booth for some free snickerdoodles, Hanan whispered to me, "These are good and all, but I heard that there aren't any dishwashers in the home economics kitchens. All the dishes have to be washed *by hand*. No thanks."

And when I dared to glance at the Math Olympiad's display, Hanan grabbed me by my sleeve and yanked me away.

"Are you *insane?*" she hissed. "Competitive mathematics? *Seriously?*"

"Did you not see their trifold?" I snapped back. "They went to Orlando last year. In Florida!"

"I'm pretty sure there's only one Orlando, Wesley. And trust me, it isn't worth it."

"Trust *me*, you're only saying that because you've been there so many times. Your family goes on vacation every year. I've never even flown on a plane!"

"You're not joining the math team. Not on my watch."

"You're making it sound like a death sentence," I said. "I bet it wouldn't be so bad. I like math."

"Okay, but this isn't actually about math, is it? Or Orlando, for that matter." Hanan shot me a scorching look. "You're just trying to find some place to fit in. You want to define yourself: Wesley the Gamer, Wesley the Cheerleader, Wesley the Mathlete."

"What are you even talking about?" I asked, bristling.

"But what you're looking for—it's not going to come from a club in school. It has to come from here," she said, stabbing me in the middle of my chest with her fingertips. Bruising me directly over my heart.

I flinched away from her. "*Ow*. But thanks, I guess. You sound like a movie character."

"You're welcome," she answered, not picking up on my sarcasm.

"I must have misunderstood, because I thought we both wanted to join a club together. For fun. But apparently, I'm desperate to fit in and you're just feeling sorry for me? Is that it?"

She sighed. "Wesley."

"And if that's how you really feel, then *fine*. I don't need you to sign up for anything with me! And you know what? Maybe I *will* become a mathlete."

I stormed off before she could open her smart mouth again. And in that moment, I really did plan to return to the Math Olympiad's booth.

But then, another club's display caught my eye.

17

The Native/Indigenous Student Union was led by
Ms. Gilbert. She teaches Honors English for eighth
graders, and I've heard that some people sign up
for it just for the chance to be in her class. Everyone seems to like her, and when I approached her
at the club fair, it was easy to see why.

Ms. Gilbert had an open, friendly face. She had
lightly tanned skin, a smattering of brown freckles, and bright-white teeth. Her black hair was
styled in a wavy bob with violet streaks. Her elab-
orate dentalium shell earrings were long enough to
graze the tops of her shoulders. She wore a sharp,

fitted blazer and black jeans, and her fingers were covered in silver rings with turquoise pendants.

"Hello there," she said, extending a hand to me. "Gaia Gilbert. Chumash. Welcome."

"Hi. Wesley Wilder." I hesitated, unsure if I should name my background, since I wasn't technically affiliated with any tribe.

Ms. Gilbert's smile warmed her brown eyes. "Nice to meet you, Wesley. These are our club leaders, Armando and Autumn."

Like in every other club, both leaders were eighth graders. As a new seventh grader on campus, I'd never met them before, but they both seemed very nice.

Armando was tall and broad, big enough to pass as a high schooler. His black hair was buzzed on the sides, slightly longer on the top of his head. His skin was dark brown. He wore rectangular glasses and a purple football jersey. His joyful grin emphasized the pudginess in his cheeks, and the gleam in his eyes was so happy and pure, it was impossible not to smile back at him.

"Hey," he said, as we shook hands. "Yakama and Colville on my mom's side; Mexican and African on my dad's."

Autumn's hair was dyed a burnished, caramelly

gold, but her roots were coming in dark brown. Her skin was deep bronze. When she smiled at me, I noticed that she had braces, and as we shook hands, I also noticed that she had written several reminders to herself in ink across her palm and the inside of her wrist.

"Quinault," she told me. "Are you new here?"

"I am," I said. "I'm a seventh grader."

"And how are you enjoying Shorelands?" Ms. Gilbert asked excitedly.

We chatted for a little bit. If any of them thought it was weird that I didn't declare myself as a member of any particular tribe, they were polite enough not to say so. And when I added my name and student email address to the short roster on Ms. Gilbert's clipboard, all three of them seemed genuinely delighted.

"We're going to meet every other Monday during lunch in my classroom," Ms. Gilbert said. "We have a bunch of cool stuff planned. I'll explain it all in the introductory email!"

"Can't wait to get to know you better," Autumn said.

"See you later!" Armando added.

I left their booth feeling uplifted and vindicated. It was especially nice, considering the argument

I'd had with Hanan. My best friend was a strong-willed, independent person, and I loved those things about her, but it seemed like we couldn't find a club to join together.

Which was fine. It really was.

A few days later, a message from Ms. Gilbert popped up in my inbox:

Hi all,

Happy Thursday! I hope your school year is off to a great start. Is everyone enjoying their classes? Making new friends?

Unfortunately, I'm reaching out with some sad news. Our application to form the Native/Indigenous Student Union has been rejected by the school administration. According to them, all officially sanctioned school clubs require a minimum of five members, two club leaders, and one teacher to supervise the club's activities. In our case, three students in addition to our two leaders signed up to join us at the club fair.

In my opinion, this rejection is both silly and ridiculous. If a group of likeminded students want to get together and create a community, they should have the freedom and support to do so, regardless of how big or small their club is. In the spirit of this personal belief, I want to keep my classroom space open to you all, along with a standing invitation to continue on with the NISU in an unofficial capacity. We might not have a designated page in the school yearbook or the ability to host or sponsor club-affiliated events on campus, but that doesn't mean we can't have our own fun!

Please think it over. I was very much looking forward to getting to know you all. I hope you won't feel deterred or overly disappointed in the administration's decision.

Sincerely,

GG

18

As Hanan and I leave Ms. Roux's classroom, each of us toting tall stacks of newspapers down the ramp that runs alongside the portable, my mind meanders, sifting through all these thoughts and memories.

And I must be a little too quiet for a little too long, because Hanan peeks at me and asks, "You okay, Wes?"

"Yeah," I say, with a quick smile. A short nod. "I'm good."

She watches me for a moment, but she doesn't press any further.

"Okay," she says. "I'll take my papers to the library; you bring yours to the SUB. They go on the shelf under the big bulletin board. Cool?"

"Sounds good. See you at lunch? After I do—the thing."

Hanan beams and says, "Yep! Good luck! You've totally got this, girl."

I tell her, "Thanks," and then we split off in opposite directions.

By the time I reach the SUB—otherwise known as the student union building, where there are bulletin boards and couches and vending machines—there are only a few minutes left before the first bell.

I drop my stack of newspapers on the shelf. A group of North Shore eighth graders are huddled around the orange sofa in the middle of the room; a boy I recognize from my math class swipes his student ID at one of the vending machines to purchase an apple juice. I linger for a moment, pretending to check the announcements on the bulletin board, waiting to see if any of them will come grab copies of the paper.

But when the bell rings, they all disperse without a single glance my way.

I follow the flow of traffic into the hallway. The

main corridor echoes with the metallic clangs of slammed lockers, the buzz of voices, and the shrill burst of a whistle, as Coach Janet snaps at someone for having their phone in their hand.

"The first bell has rung!" Coach Janet shouts. "Cell phones and personal electronics will be confiscated if I see them again! This is your final warning!"

There are hand-painted Tolo posters plastered across the walls, and green printouts taped to random lockers, advertising the Drama Club's production of *Li'l Abner*. I hurry down the hall, weaving between clusters of people, anxious to get to class on time.

I reach my classroom and take my seat in the middle row, and the final bell rings within moments. As usual, I sit through roll call, stand for the Pledge of Allegiance, and listen to the morning announcements over the intercom. I wait to see if our student council president, Christian Barrera, will mention Indigenous Peoples' Day, but he doesn't; he simply gives a shout-out to the cross-country team for their upcoming race on Wednesday, and he congratulates the debate team for winning their match last Friday.

Then something surprising happens.

There is a burst of noise in the background; the mic picks up on the feedback, and all the kids in my class wince and cry out and cover their ears. Christian pauses midsentence, and we have no idea what's happening. We can tell that someone has entered the room, and that they are now speaking to Christian, but their words are garbled.

A boy in the back of the classroom shouts, "It's the aliens! They're coming for us!"

Our first-period teacher, Ms. Nelson, shoots him a glare for being disruptive.

We hear Christian huff a breath. He chuckles slightly into the mic.

There are cheers and applause in the back ground.

"Well, uh," Christian says. "I guess we have one more announcement this morning: I am going to Tolo with Wren Wilson."

The cheering intensifies, and several people start clapping in my own classroom.

I clap along with them, even though I don't know Christian or Wren personally.

Ms. Nelson starts her lecture, but as I lift my pencil to take notes, my mind wanders and my stomach flutters. I think of Ryan's sun-bright smile and his honey-gold hair. I think of him giving me a thumbs-up after I explained the reasons why I love *Spacefaring Wanderers*. I hear his voice in my head: *Do you mind if I sit here?*

I feel the soft, warm glow of hope in my heart and refuse to let it go.

19

My second class of the day is science with Ms. Aguilar. The moment I walk in, I sense that something is different—from the volume of my classmates' voices, and from their fizzy, frantic energy. I stop and look around and promptly realize what it is.

We have a new seating chart.

"*Students*," Ms. Aguilar calls out. "Calm yourselves. Find your name and have a seat."

Her words are like a scythe through wheat, slicing through the noise, silencing the crowd.

I join the quiet huddle at the front of the room. Between the taller heads and shoulders, I glimpse my name on the piece of paper taped to the white-board. My new seat is in the far back corner of the room, beside—Skye Reynolds. The new girl.

Technically, all seventh graders at Shorelands are new, but Skye is new to the school district. She moved here from another state, and although I've heard some of the stories about her, I can never remember where she's from—Ohio? Oklahoma? I'm pretty sure it was an "O" state, and I also know it couldn't have been Oregon, because when Ms. Aguilar asked the class if anyone was new to the Pacific Northwest on our first day of school, Skye raised her hand.

"We have more cloudy days than rainy ones, and if you listen to any of the local radio stations, you're guaranteed to hear Nirvana at some point. So there you go," Ms. Aguilar had said, as if that summed up the basics of living near Seattle. "Wel-come to Washington State."

I take my seat. Slap my notebook down on the black tabletop. By the time the bell rings, my class-mates are all in their new seats, and Ms. Aguilar has started to pass out worksheets for today's lab assignment.

"Today," Ms. Aguilar says, "we will be exper-imenting with sidewalk chalk and vinegar. But before we begin, I'd like to take a moment to talk about the significance of this day."

I perk up, expecting her to acknowledge Indigenous Peoples' Day. Maybe she'll even give my column in the paper a shout-out. Maybe she'll say something about the Tulalip Tribes, whose reservation borders and ancestral waters are within a few miles of our school's campus.

She stands at the front of the room. Crosses her arms over her chest.

Ms. Aguilar is one of the more frightening teachers on campus. Hawkeyed and raven-haired, she comes to school each day in flawless makeup and spotless pantsuits. She doesn't tolerate troublemakers or rudeness; she has clear rules and codes of conduct in her classroom, and she doesn't play favorites or socialize with her students. There is no way to get on her "good side," but she doesn't really have a "bad side," either.

She is strict. She has high expectations and a mean stare and a lightning-crack voice, and she isn't afraid to use them.

"As of today," she says, "we are officially halfway through the first trimester. This means that your first midterm exam is coming up on Friday. Today's lab will be the final lesson on acids and bases; the rest of the week will be dedicated to review work and test preparation for this unit. There will be no homework assignments to turn in, but that is *only* because I expect *everyone* to be studying at home. Is that clear?"

This is the moment when the classroom door opens and Skye Reynolds walks in.

She looks—off.

There are pinkish smears across the lower half of her face. Her lips look unnaturally red and puffy, like she might have been wearing lipstick earlier and has since wiped it away with a napkin. Her T-shirt is awkwardly oversized, and its green fabric looks faded and worn. It doesn't match the rest of her outfit, which includes shiny black leggings and black platform boots. Her auburn hair is styled in two neat braids, intricately laced with black and red ribbons.

As she crosses the room, heading to her old seat, I can't help but notice how she keeps her gaze glued to the floor in front of her. And how her eyes also look puffy and red—as if she's been crying.

Ms. Aguilar snaps, "Skye Reynolds."

Skye stops short, her left boot chirping against the glossy tiled floor. Her shoulders curve inward as she looks up, her blue eyes wide and wounded and strangely distant.

What happened to her?

Ms. Aguilar must wonder the same thing, because the corners of her mouth soften, and her voice turns quieter and smoother as she says, "New seating chart today. You're in the back beside Wesley Wilder."

Skye turns, scanning the room, and I lift my hand in a wave. As soon as she knows where she's supposed to go, her gaze drops again, and her footsteps clomp as she hurries to our newly assigned corner.

20

As far as science lab partners go, Skye seems okay so far. We take turns and divide our tasks evenly; she has clear, easy-to-read handwriting. Her voice is so timid, it can be hard to hear her over the general buzz of classroom noise as everyone works around us. But aside from that, I'm happy with this new arrangement.

It seems like something happened to her before class, though. I'm just not sure what that something was.

And since we don't really know each other, I

don't know how to bring it up. If she even wants to talk about it at all.

We finish our work. We turn in the lab assignment. And in the final minute before the dismissal bell, right after Ms. Aguilar grants everyone permission to pack up for the day, she points at our table.

"Skye Reynolds," she shouts. "A word, please."

I hear Skye's sharp intake of breath before she stands to cross the room. I watch her go, wondering what Ms. Aguilar will say to her.

The bell rings. I leave along with everyone else, and as the heavy classroom door eases shut behind me, I glance over my shoulder just in time to see Ms. Aguilar wrap one arm around Skye's shoulders in a reassuring hug.

Here is everything I have heard and observed about Skye Reynolds:

She has dark red hair. Light, peachy skin. Blue eyes.

She often sits alone in the library at lunch.

On a school spirit day called Sports Day, she came to class wearing a sky-blue jersey with orange and white lettering, the word *Thunder* spelled across her chest. I don't watch basketball, so I didn't understand the reference, but I did overhear my English teacher, Mr. Holt, jokingly complain about how Skye "stole them from us." Which must mean that her team beat his in a championship. Or something like that.

And of course, there was also the rumor that spread about her, which claimed that Skye was either suspended or expelled from her last school. A few weeks ago, it was all anyone in our grade seemed to be talking about. But the details were murky; the actual origins of the story were unclear. No one was able to agree on any particular version of the story, from whether Skye had been kicked out after a fight, or a political statement, or a dress-code violation.

During the bus ride home one day, I asked Hanan about it. In response, she sighed and shook her head.

"You don't actually believe any of that, do you?"

"I'm not sure what to believe anymore," I answered honestly.

"People just like to talk," Hanan said. "Everyone loves a good controversy. And they love to have opinions about things without bothering to know any real facts at all." She crossed her arms over her chest. "I think the nosy jerks in this school should leave the new girl alone."

"Yeah," I agreed. "You're probably right."

Our conversation ended there, and as the days wore on, the attention of the entire seventh grade shifted. There were new rumors, new events on campus, new discussions and whispers and opinions all the time. There have even been some other new kids since the school year started—a boy who returned to public school after his hybrid home-schooling program didn't work out; a girl whose family moved here from the Bay Area in California last week.

And despite the rumors of disobedience and possible expulsion, Skye has never caused any real trouble here. As far as I can tell, she is a shy, quiet girl, who hasn't made many friends in our school yet.

Maybe in class tomorrow, I should make a bigger effort to talk to her.

21

Carrying on.

I go to my classes. I daydream and zone out and walk around feeling jittery all morning. Each time the bell rings, my stomach swoops like I'm approaching the peak in a roller coaster. And as the lunch hour creeps closer, as hungry gurgles stir in my belly, as I try to focus on my teachers' lectures—I start to lose my nerve.

Can I do this? Am I really going to ask him? Is this happening?

I am torn between wanting to sprint to the computer lab at lunchtime and wanting to hide forever.

And everyone seems obsessed with that Pan-thers Tolo Predictions account. Which really isn't helping.

"Did you guys see the new posts?" Emi Chan asked our table group in geography, when we were all supposed to be labeling a map of Central Amer-ica. "*Look.*"

She checked to make sure our teacher was occu-pied before sliding her phone to the center of the table. Jagged cracks splintered across the middle of its screen, and she had to turn the brightness up for us to see the social media page clearly.

Two new pictures had been added to the top row of the grid, above the colored squares. The first was of a boy and girl I didn't recognize, standing shoulder-to-shoulder and grinning beneath a dis-play of giant, golden letter balloons that spelled the word *TOLO*. The next was of Christian Barrera and Wren Wilson smiling in the front office; Chris-tian proudly held a bouquet of red roses.

Emi pulled her phone back, hiding it inside her sparkly pencil case.

All morning long, it has been like that. Every-one keeps talking about it. Swapping theories about who created the account. Placing bets on which predictions are most likely to come true.

Meanwhile, I'm trying not to think about it. Trying not to dwell on the fact that someone paired Ryan with Ella. Or that they didn't bother to pair me with anyone at all.

It's okay, I tell myself. *It doesn't mean anything. It doesn't matter.*

The bell rings.

Lunch hour begins.

I'm not nervous or anything. Nope. Not at all, no.

(Gulp.)

I gather my things and zip up my backpack and make my way toward the door. My teacher, Ms. Johansson, is calling out final instructions and homework reminders, despite the rapid surge of students leaving the room, the rise of chatter and voices and noises echoing up and down the hallway.

My seat is in the back of the classroom once again, so I'm among the last to leave, but I stop short by the recycling bin beside the door. Because right there, in the open blue tray, is an entire stack of the *Shorelands Times*. The newspapers are neatly folded and look undisturbed, just as they did in Ms. Roux's room this morning, when they'd arrived fresh from the printer.

I hesitate. Glance back at Ms. Johansson.

She settles in at her desk with a sigh. Drops a meager brown paper bag onto the tabletop in front of her. Pushes her glasses up onto her forehead to rub at her eyes fervently with the backs of her knuckles.

After a long moment, she readjusts her glasses. Reaches for her lunch.

Then she notices me. Blinks once. Sighs again.

"Can I help you with something, Winnie?"

I bristle at the incorrect name, even though it's not the first time this has happened. There is a seventh grader named Winnie, who also happens to be a light-skinned, long-haired brunette. Just like me. We both have dark hair and light-brown eyes. We are close to the same height. And she's the first chair violin in orchestra, which means that she carries an instrument case to school that looks a lot like mine. So for people who glimpse us from behind, or who don't know us very well, I can see how it would be easy to mix us up.

But still. I've been in her class since the first week of September; you'd think that Ms. Johansson would know who I am by now.

"I, uh—sorry," I say, though I'm not sure what I'm sorry for. "Are these supposed to be in here?" I pick up a copy of the newspaper.

"Oh," she says wearily. "Those. Please, take one if you want. Ms. Roux always sends me way too many of those things."

All I can think to say is, "Oh. Okay."

I swing my backpack around in front of me. Unzip the large pouch and tuck this unread newspaper into the mesh interior pocket, along with the first copy that I held this morning.

Then I leave.

22

Lunchtime.

I'm so excited and nervous and queasy, it takes all of my concentration to bite into the apple that Mom packed in my snack box. It's tart and crisp, and each crunching chew sounds *extremely* loud in my head, but I don't want my stomach to rumble when I approach Ryan in the computer lab, and there's also no way I'm ready for a full meal from the cafeteria yet, so here I am.

Eating an apple.

Walking down the hallway.

Definitely not overthinking.

I turn the corner, following the curved wall that wraps around the backside of the library and connects to the computer lab. There aren't any lockers in this corner of the campus, and the small classrooms along this path are used for special education services and study halls, so it's quiet here. Empty. The wall to my left features a painted mural of jade-green jungle leaves, framed around a prowling black panther, and followed by the words *Shorelands Strong* in purple-and-gold calligraphy. To my right, the beige-painted wall is filled with Tolo posters, school spirit day reminders, and a gallery of charcoal drawings created by an art class.

I pause for a second. Up ahead, there is a bank of windows that peer into the lab. Even from this distant angle, I can see the bluish-white glow of the screens. The door is also propped open, and I can hear the trilling *rat-tat-tat* of an alien spaceship battle, the encouraging sound of Mr. Li's voice.

He's probably there. Seated at Computer #7.

(Gulp!)

Before I fully grasp what I'm doing, I'm pivoting on my heel and circling back the way I came, chomping and gnawing at the shiny pink-green skin of the apple as I move. My heart feels like it's about to gallop straight out of my chest. My feet carry me farther and farther away, until I reach the more populated part of this hallway, near the entrance to the library.

I plop down on a bench beside the book return chute.

Deep breaths, I think, dragging in a lungful of air.

Once, my grandfather told me: *The things that scare us the most in this world are usually the most worthwhile things in our lives.* We were watching a horror film about a haunted house with a moonlit cornfield at the time, and he was trying to convince me to pay attention and stop hiding behind my hands. But I'd like to think that his advice applies to moments like this, too.

I just like Ryan so much. I think he's funny. He's smart. He's kind and considerate. In the Gamer Club, he has this way of talking to everyone and bringing people together, to make sure everybody feels included. And he wears that purple bracelet that his sister made for him every single day. I've never seen him without it.

He also has great hair. And an all-around cute face.

And yet, as good-looking as he is, it's his personality that makes him the most attractive boy in the entire seventh grade.

So yes, I'm nervous. I'm a little bit afraid.

But it's only because he's worth it.

I take another deep breath. Toss my apple core into the garbage. Gather up my courage. I pull my backpack into my lap, unzip the wide pouch, whisk out my binder and one copy of the newspaper. I glance around. There are a few people milling about—some eighth graders exchanging contact information, a janitor rolling a giant bin down the hallway—but none of them are paying any attention to me.

Carefully, I slide the card free from the binder's interior flap. I open the newspaper to page seven and place it there, folding it in. Then I tuck everything into my backpack, doing my best not to crumple the papers.

I zip the pouch.

Rise from the bench.

And set off back down the hall.

I follow the curved wall, and in my head, I'm rehearsing the lines: *Ryan, did you see that you were mentioned in the paper today? Yes, you were! Turn to page seven.*

Over and over, again: *Ryan, did you see that you were mentioned in the paper today?*

I pass by the painting of the panther. I peek up at the words *Shorelands Strong.* I knead my hands together as I approach the end of the corridor, the wide bank of windows and the blue-white glare of computer screens, the invitation of the open door.

And then—

A classroom door whips open behind me, startling me. I whirl around and lock eyes with a girl who freezes at the sight of me. It's clear that she didn't expect anyone to be out here, just as I'd assumed all of these classrooms were empty.

It's also clear that she has been crying.

She mutters a quick "Sorry," and turns, hurrying down the hall and disappearing inside the nearby girls' bathroom.

I stare after her, shocked and momentarily unsure of what to do.

This is the second time I've encountered a girl who seemed visibly upset today.

This is the second time I've wondered how to handle this sort of situation. Especially since we're not friends. We've never really spoken before. We don't know each other well at all.

I look at the open door to the computer lab.

I look at the closed door to the girls' bathroom.

And even though I'm feeling hesitant, and this whole lunch hour hasn't gone according to plan so far, I can't make myself turn away from her.

So I follow Ella Holland.

23

The bathroom door doesn't give me a stealthy entrance.

Its hinges squeak and rattle and groan, it rasps as it sweeps against the tiled floor, and as I step inside, the door slides shut with a firm slap.

This is a bathroom with dark-gray walls, three gleaming sinks and mirrors, and three stalls. No one else is in here. Ella Holland's candy-pink sneakers with mint-green laces are the only shoes visible beneath the gaps. She is standing in the third stall, with her back to the door.

I can hear her sniffling. Soft and muffled, like she's trying to stop herself.

"Hello?"

Silence.

One of the faucets randomly drips. In the hallway outside, I hear the unmistakable rumble of the janitor pushing their giant bin back down the corridor.

I swallow. Take another step forward. "Ella?" It feels weird to address her by name when we've never formally met, but I decide my own discomfort is irrelevant. "Are you okay?"

I watch as she shifts her weight, leaning forward and rising up on her toes, then tilting back onto her heels.

"Is there anything I can do to help?" I ask. "I can—I can go get someone? If you want?"

There's another beat of silence.

Then the gentle scuff of her sneakers as she turns around. The click of the bolt as she unlocks the stall door.

She steps out slowly.

Ella doesn't wear much makeup—just a touch of mascara, sometimes winged eyeliner. Since she has been crying, her blue eyes are underlined in black smudges, and her cheeks are stained with inky tear tracks. A lock of her blond hair is stuck to the left side of her face. Her hands clutch the straps of her rainbow-patterned backpack so tightly, her knuckles look white.

"Um. Hi," she says. Her voice sounds high and shaky. "Can you maybe watch the door while I fix— this?" She waves a hand in front of her own face.

"Sure," I say quickly. "Of course. Whatever you need."

Her shoulders sag with relief. "Thanks."

She sniffles again and shuffles over to the paper towel dispenser. It reverberates like a drum as she pulls its lever up and down. She tears herself a piece with a swift, clean rip.

"I'm, um—I'm not normally like this," she murmurs. "Just saying."

I only shrug in response.

Ella steps in front of the mirror. Dampens the paper towel. I watch as she leans forward, wiping her face and blinking rapidly at her reflection.

I ask her, "Do you want to talk about it?"

Her gaze flicks to meet mine in the mirror.

Hastily, I add, "You don't have to or anything. Obviously."

She blinks at me. Looks down at the towel in her hands. Clenches her fists.

For some reason, I can't stop talking, so I say, "Like, I'm just some random person who happened to cross your path in a—uh, a difficult moment, it seems like. So if you'd prefer to say nothing, I get that. Totally understand. Either way."

I'm babbling more than Baby Zoe.

Ella turns to me, facing me directly. The straight-faced coolness that I remember, the expression that I had always associated with her and had interpreted as snobbish, has returned. Her eyes are still a little bleary; her cheeks are pink from the coarse paper. But suddenly, she seems to be back. The girl who never smiles or slows down in the school hallways. The girl whose chin is always raised.

It makes me feel insecure. Uncertain.

But then she speaks, her voice soft and amazed as she says, "You're so nice."

I blush instantly; she takes a small step toward me.

"I'm serious," Ella says. "You might be the nicest person I've met at this school. But I'm sorry. I don't know your name."

"I'm Wesley."

"Wesley," she repeats, whispering. She gives me a tentative smile. Kneads her hands together. She raises her voice, sounding more confident. "Well,

Wesley. It's really nice to meet you."

I smile back. "It's nice to meet you, too."

"And honestly, I'm—I'm okay. I'm better now. You've already helped me a whole lot, and if you have somewhere to be . . ."

"Are you sure? Do you have anyone else to talk to?"

"Technically, yes," she says, her gaze skirting away again. "I have—friends. A lot of them, supposedly."

"But?"

"But I'm not sure if they want to hear it anymore. You don't really have to, either."

I tell her, "Try me."

24

From there, I learn a lot about Ella Holland.

I learn that her parents separated last summer. It sounds like it has been an ugly divorce, with her parents speaking to each other exclusively through written communications between their lawyers, which I had never even realized was a *thing*. I mean, I guess my own parents don't talk anymore, either. But Ella actually grew up with both of hers, so this seems different.

I also learn that she was recently diagnosed with dyslexia. Except her parents apparently disagree about whether or not her diagnosis is "real."

Her mom thinks that Ella is just distracted and needs to "try harder" in class. Her dad, on the other hand, thinks that Ella should take time away from her soccer team to work with a private tutor so she won't fall behind in school. Through their lawyers, they compromised by adding a period of study hall to Ella's schedule, even though Ella was excited about her ceramics class—an elective she no longer has time for.

And I learn that some of her "friends" don't sound like real friends at all. Just before lunch started, one of Ella's friends told her there were people in the world with "real problems."

"Ugh, why would she say that to you?"

Ella gives a dispirited shrug. "I don't know. Maybe she has a point?"

"She's wrong," I insist. "You're not overreacting or being too sensitive. You're going through *a lot* right now. Your friends should be helping you through it, not making things worse by being so mean."

She sighs. "Yeah," she admits softly. "You're probably right."

"I am. Trust me."

The bell rings, signaling the end of our lunch hour and startling us both. As if in protest of my negligence, my stomach gurgles long and loud; Ella looks at me with a shocked, sheepish expression on her face.

"Oh *no*," she cries. "Have you not eaten lunch yet? Why didn't you say anything?"

"Oops," I say, chagrined. "I, uh—kind of forgot."

"How could you forget to *eat*?"

I start to respond, but then my mind races as I think about my plan, about Ryan in the lab, about the card still waiting inside my backpack.

Ella is frantically removing the straps of her rainbow-patterned backpack. She sifts through the main pocket and pulls her metal lunchbox free; she pops its lid open, revealing half a sandwich and a small bag of carrot sticks.

"I don't have much left, but please—"

"No," I say quickly, shaking my head. "It's okay, really—"

"No, no, you spent all this time listening to me and making me feel better, and I totally robbed you of your lunch." She shoves the food at me. "It's the least I can do." Her eyes go wide. "Unless—wait, unless you're allergic to peanuts?"

"I'm not—"

"Then it's settled. Here, congratulations. A PB&J sandwich and some carrots."

I can't help but smile. "Okay," I say, accepting the offer. "Thank you. I appreciate it."

I tuck the food away in my backpack, and my cheeks go warm at the sight of the newspaper folded over the card.

In the hallway outside, there is a sharp increase in murmurs and footsteps and noise.

I zip my backpack shut and decide that maybe this was for the best. I was so nervous about asking Ryan to Tolo. Maybe I'll just give myself another day to mentally prepare. Maybe I'll wait until after our Gamer Club meeting and ask him when there are less people around on campus.

Yes. Perhaps that's what I'll do.

Ella and I exit the bathroom together. We linger just outside the door; she's going to the left, my next class is off to the right.

"So," she says. "I really enjoyed talking with you. Thanks again."

I tell her, "Anytime."

She perks up. "Do you have a cell phone? Or are you on social media?"

"No and no, unfortunately. But I have a gamertag! Do you play any video games?"

Ella's entire face brightens.

25

My afternoon classes pass in a blur.

I scarf down the sandwich and nibble on a few carrot sticks, and I'm filled with gratitude on my way to PE, because it's Monday Runday, and there's no way I would have survived without more food in my stomach. I change into my gym shirt and shorts in the locker room; it smells intensely of sweaty socks and a blend of body sprays in here, and I avoid all eye contact as I shove my regular clothes into the blue metal locker. Then I linger in the back corner for a moment, chatting with some friends until Coach Janet's whistle shrieks at us and we scurry into action, scuttling out the door.

We gather on the track outside, and I'm delightfully surprised by the sunbreaks through the clouds, the widening bands of blue sky in the distance. Despite such a misty, gray morning, it might be clear and sunny by the time we're done with school. The track's soggy red dust scuffs beneath my sneakers. Coach Janet shouts her usual instructions, then blasts her whistle again, setting us off to run a mile.

By the end of the fourth lap, I am drenched in sweat and pushing through the exhaustion, pumping my legs as fast as I can. I'm gasping, drawing the chilled autumn air into my burning chest. Coach Janet's eyes flick up to meet mine as I stagger across the finish line; she checks her stopwatch and jots a note onto her clipboard.

Her voice is curt as she says, "Good work, Wilder."

Orchestra comes next after PE. We tune our instruments, rehearse our songs for the fall concert, and receive some sheet music for the solo parts we can audition for.

Health class is after that. It's health class. That's all I have to say about it.

Then the bell chimes for our final period, which

is English for me. And I'm nervous and excited, because Mr. Holt is going to share my piece from the newspaper with our class.

I'm ready for him to call on me. I know exactly what I want to say about my poem.

Mr. Holt claps his hands and says, "Okay, kids. Monday, Monday." He strides to the front of the room, uncaps a marker, and starts to write on the whiteboard.

I scoot forward in my seat, heart racing with anticipation as I wait to address the class.

But when he turns back around, Mr. Holt launches straight into his lesson plan.

I blink a few times. Glance around the classroom. Everybody is either taking notes or texting beneath their desks as Mr. Holt drones on in his lecture. Everybody except for Skye Reynolds, who is staring out the window with her chin in her palm, a dazed look on her face. Then she seems to sense me looking at her, and her blue eyes meet mine for a single, somewhat startling moment.

I turn away. Etch today's date dutifully into the headline of my notes. And when I peek in her direction again, I see that Skye has hidden her face behind the curtain of her auburn hair.

Mr. Holt starts a new line of text on the

whiteboard. I follow the words as he writes them.

Has there been some kind of mistake? Did he not receive a copy of the newspaper today? Did he forget to call on me?

I crane my neck to examine his desk from afar, and—well, he has a copy. A few separate sheets of it are spread across his desk, so he must have read it.

I wonder why he isn't calling on me.

I try to focus on my work. Try to listen to Mr. Holt's lecture, which has something to do with subject-verb agreements in essay writing. I don't know. His words and explanations are all jumbling together in my head.

My heart keeps on racing; my palms remain slick with sweat as I fumble through my notes. I keep expecting him to remember; I keep waiting for him to pause his lecture.

But he never does.

26

By the time the final bell rings, echoing across the campus, causing classrooms to erupt, sending flurries of freed students into the halls—I gather my things and tentatively approach my teacher. I stand behind him as he clears the whiteboard. His eraser squeaks as he whisks it back and forth.

Eventually, he turns around.

Mr. Holt is wearing a checkered beige shirt, its sleeves pushed up above his elbows. His forehead gleams under the classroom lights; it reminds me of the shiny bald spot on the back of his head. A small crease forms between his brows as he says,

"Wesley. Did you have a question about the home-work assignment?"

"Actually, I, um—well, you see, I was in the paper today." I swallow. Lift my chin. "The school newspaper. And I was hoping to talk about it in class, but you never called on me, so I wanted to check in and see if you knew. That I wrote an opin-ion piece. A poem, to be exact. Maybe you didn't get a chance to read the Student Opinion section yet?"

There is a long, awkward silence. I can hear the muffled noise of students moving down the hallway outside. The low buzz of a fluorescent bulb flicker-ing overhead.

"Ah," he says neutrally. "Right." Mr. Holt crosses his arms over his chest. Tilts his head at me. "I did read the paper today. I read your piece, in fact. And if I'm being honest, Wesley, I was surprised. Very surprised."

Surprised? Really?

"Oh," I begin. "Um. Yeah, I know, it's kind of hard to tell from looking at me. Most people don't know that I'm Native, and they don't really guess it, either—"

He holds one hand up, stopping me. "That's not what I meant. As a creative writing piece, I think it was lovely. The poetic devices were great and all, there was some powerful repetition and imagery, but—to me, it felt a little bit like a missed opportunity."

My blood runs cold. I feel very small, very suddenly.

"A mi-missed opportunity?"

Mr. Holt starts to respond, but then the intercom turns on with a loud beep. He stops with a closed-lipped smile as the announcement begins, the secretary's voice crackling over the speaker in Mr. Holt's room: *This is a reminder that all eighth-grade football players and cheerleaders should board bus number ninety-three for their away game today. Again, all eighth-grade football players and cheerleaders, please board bus ninety-three for your away game. Thank you!*

Mr. Holt gives a wistful sigh. "They're playing against Wildwood tonight. Our nemesis."

I'm still standing here, staring. Feeling hollow.

"Anyway, Wesley." He taps his index finger against his chin. "In my mind, a student opinion piece about Indigenous Peoples' Day would have been a real opportunity to show a journalistic angle, to *engage* the reader and craft an argument. A dialogue. I would have liked to see more ambition from you, Wesley, perhaps in the form of a persuasive essay, rather than a poem. This is a hot topic, after all. Why *should* this new holiday replace Columbus Day?"

He gestures to me, holding one hand out as if he is gripping an invisible microphone, waiting for me to answer the question. To fill in the blank.

But in the poem, I never even mentioned Columbus Day. I didn't want to start any arguments or controversies.

I only wanted to celebrate Indigenous Peoples' Day.

"I—I guess I didn't think of it like that," I admit.

"Such a shame," he says. Then when he sees the look on my face, he's quick to add, "It was a beautiful poem, of course. But if you read my syllabus more *carefully*, you'll notice that I only give extra-credit points to students who publish in the school newspaper with *clear* thesis statements." He shrugs. "Your piece had none. It didn't choose one side of an argument; it didn't offer pros and cons, or even acknowledge the opposition at all. I'm sorry, Wesley. But I didn't share your work with the class today because you didn't follow the guidelines necessary to warrant it."

27

I'm crushed.

I don't want to be. I know it's not the end of the world, that I'll survive without the extra-credit points, but I feel like I've failed. Like I was wrong. Like submitting to the paper at all was a huge mistake.

All day long, I waited with a glimmer of hope in my heart, thinking that someone might come to me and tell me that they read my column. That it made them reflect, or it made them happy, or it intrigued them somehow. I worked so hard on it, and I felt vulnerable but excited to see my ideas in print, distributed all across the school's campus. And when that never happened, when none of my friends or classmates or anybody said anything about it to me, I figured it was okay. Because at least I would have a chance to talk about it in Mr. Holt's class. At least then, I would be able to stand up and say a few words about today's holiday.

A holiday no one in this school seems to care about. A holiday that didn't receive any special announcements or events or posters in the hallways. A holiday that has been completely ignored. Or forgotten.

And now, here I am. Walking back to the bus at the end of the day. Lugging my viola case at my side. The air is crisp and breezy in the long shadows cast by the school building at my back, but I make my way through the thinning crowd and into the sunshine. There is a packed line of yellow buses idling in the bus loop, their exhaust pipes rattling and gusting hot air around my calves as I hurry down the row. Dried leaves swirl in the air currents and crunch beneath my feet. The clasps on my viola case click and clack as my feet pound across the smooth pavement.

I find my bus and climb aboard, nodding hello to our afternoon driver. Then I hoist my viola case up awkwardly in front of me, clutching it against my chest as I shuffle down the aisle.

Hanan is back in our usual seat, waiting for me and watching my progress with a guarded look on her face.

"Hey," I rasp, dropping down beside her. "Wow. It got way too hot, way too fast."

Hanan sort of nods and shrugs in response, an uneasy twitch of her head and shoulders.

"Sorry I never met up with you at lunch," I continue on, as I set my viola case down at our feet, pull my backpack off, and start to shrug out of my sweatshirt. It was warm outside, but it's approximately a million degrees in here. "So I know what you're about to say." Hanan's brows jump slightly in alarm, and I tell her, "And no, I didn't get a chance to ask Ryan about the Tolo today, like I'd planned. But it's okay. I'm going to ask him after our Gamer Club meeting tomorrow or something instead. You're not going to believe this, but I actually spent almost the *entire* lunch hour with Ella Holland, of all people. I saw her and she was having a rough day, so we talked, and I think we might be friends now? Can you believe it? She plays *Spacefaring Wanderers* too, so we'll have to add her to our group and do a quest with her sometime."

Hanan is having a hard time meeting my gaze. I pause and pitch forward, but she turns sheepishly away from me. Then, suddenly, I realize that she hasn't spoken to me at all. Not a single word since I sat down.

Which is *very* abnormal for Hanan, my loud and extroverted and opinionated best friend.

"What's wrong?"

She bites her bottom lip. Looks at me, worried.

"Hanan?" I ask. "Are you okay? Did something happen?"

The silence stretches on a bit longer. Things continue to happen all around us: The bus door slaps shut. Our driver shouts something at the eighth graders in the back rows. The boy in the seat in front of us unlatches his window, the glass pane squeaking loudly as he drops it down.

Hanan glances away from me. Her phone screen brightens in her palms, and her thumbs flick and tap across its gleaming surface.

Then she holds it up to me. To show me.

It's another update from the Panthers Tolo Predictions account. Another new photo added to the top of their feed. And in this picture, which was taken in the courtyard outside the school cafeteria, Saylor May Rasmussen and Ryan Thomas are standing together, side by side. Saylor May is smiling and pointing at Ryan's wrist, which he is holding up in front of his face.

For as long as I have known him, Ryan has always worn his *EVILO* bracelet. A purple beaded bracelet strung with letter blocks from a child's craft kit. That same bracelet is wrapped around his suntanned skin in this picture.

But there is another bracelet stacked on top of it. A new string of purple-and-gold beads and letter blocks. And its letters spell *TOLO*.

28

This moment doesn't seem real.

It can't be real. It can't happen like this.

Hanan finally breaks her silence to say, "I'm so sorry, Wesley."

Our bus is rolling forward, ambling along in the long line of traffic, jolting over a speed bump before we pull onto the main road. Hanan's phone is still in my palms, and I accidentally brush the photo with my thumb, dragging it down to refresh the feed and update the increased number of heart reactions and congratulatory comments.

Hanan is gentle as she takes her phone back,

easing it out of my numb grip. A blast of fresh air surges through the open window ahead of us, the breeze cool against my flushed skin and stinging eyes. I blink several times, fighting against the hot, gathering tears.

Without saying a word, Hanan wraps her arms around me and pulls me into a firm hug. She presses her cheek against the top of my head, gently pats my shoulder with one hand. She holds me close, even as the bus jostles us in our seat.

She holds me up, while everything falls apart.

We sit like that, saying nothing, until the bus gets close to Hanan's stop. As we turn and glide down her street, Hanan squeezes my shoulder and pulls back.

She says, "If it makes you feel any better, I got Hannah'd *twice* today."

I give a strained giggle. "No way," I say. "By who?"

"The first time was a sub," she tells me. "Which is kind of excusable, but also not? How can you not tell the difference between an *h* and an *n*? And the second time was in the cafeteria, when the lady at the register snatched a cup of yogurt out of my hand, because of my lunch debt. It was so stupid and embarrassing. *Tell your mom to add money to your account so you can keep buying food at school, Hannah.*"

I shudder. "She needs to be careful of what she asks for. Imagine your mom's reaction when she hears about the person who snatched food out of her daughter's hand. And called you by the wrong name."

Hanan mirrors my shudder.

"Do you want some carrots?" I ask, remembering the food that Ella shared with me.

I dig around in my backpack for them, as the bus rolls to a stop outside a cul-de-sac. Hanan happily accepts the small plastic bag, and while she crunches a carrot stick, I tell her about how Ms. Johansson called me Winnie today.

Hanan makes a face. "Seriously? But you and Winnie don't look anything alike."

I shrug. "Some people disagree, I guess."

"Some people need to get their vision checked."

"And Mr. Holt didn't like my poem."

"What?"

"He didn't even give me extra credit. He said it didn't have a thesis statement. That it was a missed opportunity."

"Missed opportunity. Missed? *Opportunity?* He

really said those words to you?" Hanan shakes her head, her hazel eyes burning, suddenly enraged. "He's wrong. He's so deeply wrong, I'm actually kind of embarrassed for him. Your poem was beautiful. You wrote from the heart, and it showed."

Her praise makes me smile a little. "But maybe he had a point? Maybe I should have just written an essay and turned it into an argument. Indigenous Peoples' Day versus Columbus Day. That sort of thing."

Hanan scrunches her nose. "No. No, you didn't need to. That's not what your piece was about. At all."

"But maybe—"

"Stop it, no. Okay? Your poem was perfect. End of story."

"It didn't even have a thesis statement."

Hanan groans and drags one hand down the length of her face as she says, "Of course it did, you dummy. It's literally the title. *We still belong*— that's a thesis statement. That sums up the entire thing."

I swallow. Drop my gaze to my lap.

Hanan nudges my arm. "Look. Everyone is always looking for an argument. A debate. A fight. And sure, there are plenty of fights to be had in this world. There are some things we need to fight against, and even more things worth fighting and standing up for. It's important, but . . . we don't need to argue about every single little thing. It's not our job to go back and forth *all the time*. We can just—be. We can exist and feel proud and satisfied with ourselves. We can create art. We can celebrate. We can shut up and enjoy life, you know? Instead of constantly battling against everyone and everything, especially those who try to tell us we're not enough."

I lift my head. Our eyes lock as the bus slows, its brakes whining loudly as we approach Hanan's stop.

"You are enough, Wesley. You always have been. You have nothing to prove to Mr. Holt, or to anyone else. I mean, look at you. You're a gamer and a poet and a good friend. You're kind and funny and nerdy and weird."

"I was also almost a mathlete."

She ignores this. "You named your cat after an intergalactic supervillain with serious respiratory issues. You sing nursery rhymes to your baby cousin. Whenever you eat dinner at my house, you always help with cleaning up and putting the dishes away, so you're basically my mom's favorite person.

Which is why she always wants to play cards with us, just saying. She thinks you're the best."

My breath hitches in my chest.

I'm speechless.

"And she's right," Hanan goes on. "You *are* the best. And if Mr. Holt couldn't see how great your poem was, and how it captured so many things about you and your family and your heritage and the world, that's his problem. Not yours."

At the moment, all I can do is offer a feeble nod in response.

We both rise, and I step into the aisle, allowing Hanan to squeeze by me. She gives me a pointed look as she steps over my viola case, her hazel eyes lit with triumph.

"And by the way," she says, "I *knew* you'd like Ella Holland once you gave her a chance. Totally called that one."

29

After Hanan leaves and the bus pulls forward again, I feel the weight of this entire day settle over me. Crushing me.

I draw my legs up, placing my feet on the vinyl seat, hugging my knees against my chest. I sniffle and stare out the window, feeling lonely and uncertain. I try to hold the warmth of Hanan's words in my heart, but without my best friend here beside me, coldness creeps in.

When we reach my stop, I carry my viola down the aisle, thank the driver as I always do, and step out into the surprising heat of a golden autumn afternoon. But even with my sweatshirt tied around my waist, and the sunlight drenching my surroundings, the coldness follows me all the way home.

There are no cars outside Grandpa's house, which is wildly unusual. But it's also nice, because it means that no one is here to notice as I march straight down the driveway and around to the side of the house, where we keep our waste collection bins. I unzip my backpack, flip my binder open, remove the card that I made for Ryan—and drop it straight into the recycling bin. Then, for good measure, I crumple up both copies of the school newspaper and dump them in, too.

I'm pretty sure no one aside from Hanan and Mr. Holt and Ms. Roux read my column, anyway.

My face feels overheated. My stomach writhes with squeamishness. I let my backpack and viola case clatter to the floor, kick my shoes off by the overflowing shoe rack, and go collapse on the couch. I reach for my console controller, the remote control—all I want right now is to do a few quests in *Spacefaring Wanderers* and try to forget about it. All of it.

The TV screen brightens. There is a swell of

soothing music as the lobby menu loads, filling the screen with stars and galaxy swirls, and rippling shades of purple and indigo and blue. I open the map, revealing a collection of colorful planets, the dashed rings of their orbits. They almost remind me of beads on bracelets, which of course makes me think of Ryan, which then makes my eyes burn and my breath hitch unevenly in my chest.

I choose the desert planet.

My spaceship touches down in a sea of pink-gold sand dunes, beside a small alien village. The locals have cactus-green skin and tower over my avatar in height. I run around their huts, haggling over prices, chatting with them to solve riddles and unlock side quests.

Vader sneaks up and hops onto the couch. He hovers by my feet, his green eyes wide and shoulders slightly hunched, his tail in the shape of a question mark. I pause the game and hold my hand out to him, wiggling my fingers. He pauses too, assessing me for a moment before he hurries forward, trotting across my legs to push his forehead to my fingertips.

"Hey," I say. "I missed you, boy. I missed you so much."

He purrs in response, deep and resonant, as he

peers up at me with squinty eyes. He rubs his nose against my palm, then sniffs my controller and pushes his cheek against it, his whiskers brushing along the buttons.

I suddenly feel the urge to cry again, but I don't bother to fight it this time. The tears slide down my splotchy cheeks. I sniffle and cough on a sob. Vader curls up in my lap, purring loudly as he nuzzles me. He stays right here, warm and affectionate and sleepy, as I send my avatar off into the dunes, in search of a hidden gem.

Grandpa comes storming through the front door. I wipe my cheeks quickly, to hide the fact that I have been crying, but he doesn't even look at me right away. Instead, he bustles over to stare expectantly at the TV.

"Hi, Grandpa," I say, as casually as I can. "How was your afternoon route?"

"It was fine. Where's the show, Wesley?" he asks urgently. "Why didn't you put the show back on? We need to see the progress on the bar!"

"Um," I say. "What show?"

"The pink kitty girl! Her show! Put her channel back on; I want to see how much money she and her friends have raised."

"Oh—*oh!* You mean gemmakitty01?"

"Gemma, the pink kitty girl, the Klamath gamer girl, that's the one. Put her on, Wesley."

"Klamath?"

"She's enrolled with the Klamath Tribes. She talked about it earlier."

"Oh. How long were you watching the stream, Grandpa?" He shoots me a withering look.

"Long enough. Now are you going to put her on, or should I just find the channel myself?"

I say, "Yes, sir," and grab the remote. He joins me on the couch, and when I start to move my feet to make room for him, he motions for me to stop.

"Can't disturb the cat," he says, as he sits and scoots in, tapping my socked feet with one hand.

I save my progress in *Spacefaring Wanderers*. Change the input on the TV. Open the streaming app. Click on gemmakitty01's feed.

And I gasp.

30

When Grandpa said, *We need to see the progress on the bar*, I'd had no idea what he was talking about. I had forgotten.

Gemma is doing an all-day charity stream for Indigenous Peoples' Day.

The donations are being tracked on a bar at the top of the screen.

And so far, she has raised $14,920.

Onscreen, Gemma is excitedly saying, "This is so unbelievable, you guys. You've almost raised *fifteen grand* for Native kids across the country. With these funds, we will be able to clear the wish lists for teachers working in reservation schools. We can send new books and toys to daycare centers. It's just unbelievable. Your generosity is beautiful." She draws a quick breath. Takes a moment to tighten her pink pigtails. When she speaks again, her voice quakes as she says, "Education is power. Joy is power. Kindness is power. Thank you all for coming here today to help us empower Native youth."

She isn't playing a game right now. She must be taking a break between appearances to chat and wait for her next guest. And since she is between games, the camera view of her room has been enlarged to fill the screen, which means we are able to clearly watch the starry-eyed emotion in her eyes when the next donation comes in: $250.

Someone just donated $250 to Gemma's charity stream.

Grandpa gives a low whistle.

Gemma presses her fingertips to her temples and says, "That's it. There we go. Fifteen grand, all for the kids."

"Wow," I murmur.

"Yep," Grandpa says. "Pretty awesome, kiddo."

I cluck my tongue and add, "Not bad for a single day of work."

Grandpa makes a sound that is somewhere between a sigh and a growl. He simply responds, "Yeah. Well."

We watch as Gemma introduces her next guest, a Tlingit man who is the lead singer of a pop rock band. Grandpa and I watch together, chuckling at their jokes. Then they start playing a gory, M-rated zombie apocalypse game.

I groan. Grandpa is going to love this. Me, not so much.

"Just a game, Wesley," Grandpa croons, as I flinch and startle and hide behind my hands. "Come on, little one, you know zombies aren't real . . ." He peeks at me, the fine lines crinkling around his brown eyes as he flashes a menacing smile. "Or should I say, they're not real *yet*."

"Ha-ha," I say halfheartedly. "You're so funny."

"Where would we go? If the zombies do, in fact, come for us someday?"

I glare at him. Grandpa laughs, reaching over to pat my knee. Vader lifts his head. His fur and whiskers are flattened against his right cheek. His green eyes are narrowed in annoyance.

"What? I'm being serious! Where would you want to go, if we ever had to evacuate and survive in the world on our own?"

"I don't know," I mutter, because this isn't exactly the sort of thing I want to think about. "A supermarket, maybe?"

Grandpa nods. "Sure. Solid choice."

"What about you?"

"Wherever my family goes, I would follow."

I pause. Give him a skeptical stare. "Is that your real answer? I don't know if that one counts."

"Why not?" he scoffs.

"Because it's obvious," I say. "Of course we'd stick together."

Grandpa regards me with a long, contemplative look. His short, salt-and-pepper hair is neatly combed. His tanned skin is age-spotted, with rays of wrinkles around the corners of his eyes and mouth. His eyelashes are short and stubby like mine, framing the light-brown eyes that I inherited. He's wearing a green flannel and dark jeans. He places his hand on my crossed ankles.

"I'm glad that seems obvious to you," he says. "I think you'd be amazed by how many people would disagree. How many people would go out and try to survive on their own, just themselves against the world. But lone wolves are usually the hungriest, Wesley. There is strength and safety in packs. In family and community."

We sit with his words for a moment. His hand is warm and comforting on my ankles.

Then a burst of noise from the TV makes me jump, just as Vader has started to lower his chin again. I'm quick to apologize, but he pins his annoyed green gaze on me without a care. He stands up, stretches his legs, and slinks off across the room without a backward glance, his tail curling haughtily behind him.

31

As we continue to watch the stream together, I start to wonder about how Grandpa survived the heartache after Grandma Denise died.

I get sad and feel like I miss her sometimes, and I barely even knew her. I have a vague memory of her waiting for me at the bottom of a playground slide with her arms wide open, beaming and calling my name as I came crashing into her embrace. But even though it feels real to me, and certain details about it seem so clear—the smell of lavender on her skin, the crunch of woodchips beneath her feet—it only comes to me in that one small snapshot. I can never picture the park we're in. Or what the weather was like that day. Or anything else about the time we must have shared together.

It's a strange thing, to miss someone you don't remember.

And apparently, Grandpa is also thinking of her, because he tells me, "Your grandmother would have gotten a real kick out of this. Have I ever told you about how she used to play *Ms. Pac-Man*?"

I smile softly. Shake my head.

"Ah, well. That woman. She was unbeatable at that game. It used to drive me insane, but I'll tell you what, Wesley—I'd give anything to let her beat me again, one last time."

His throat bobs as he swallows. His gaze remains fixed on the TV.

They were married for twenty-three years. That's almost twice as long as I've been alive. I can't imagine loving someone for so long, then losing them and having to move on.

Grandpa's voice sounds gravelly as he says, "You know, Wesley—have I ever told you about the signal?" He shifts his gaze to me and says, "The special signal that your grandmother and I shared? The one that really made her—my person? The one for me?"

Once again, I shake my head.

"Well. It was a simple thing. Some of the best things in life are small and simple, aren't they? And this was one of those . . ." He sighs, remembering. "Anyway. It happened whenever we were in a crowded room. She and I could be on the opposite sides of a gigantic space. It could be a party in someone else's house, or a festival in the middle of a field, or we could be somewhere really huge. An arena. A concert."

He grins at me, and I find myself smiling along with him. He and Grandma Denise met at a rock concert in Seattle; I've heard the story before. It's one of my favorites that he tells.

"I'd be way over here; she would be way, *way* over there—and yet, despite the distance, despite anything and everything happening around us, somehow we would always find each other. No matter what, I would find her. I could pick her out of any crowd."

I feel a lump rising in my throat. I blink back the tears before they have a chance to gather.

Grandpa says, "We could almost *sense* each other's presence. And when we'd find each other and make eye contact—there was this moment. This spark of connection." He snaps his fingers and gives a slight shudder. "That was it. The signal. I don't know how else to describe it. Every time our eyes met, I felt like I was exactly where I was supposed to be. Every time I found her in a crowd, it was like coming home."

The light from the TV flickers in Grandpa's eyes. I watch as the corners of his mouth tighten.

"After she died," he says, the gravel returning to his voice, "I was lost. It took a long time to heal. A long time to find my way back to myself. And even as my life returned to normal, I would sometimes catch myself seeking her out, searching for her eyes. For that missing signal.

"It still happens," he says. "Hits me all over again. And it hurts, but I've learned to live with it. To embrace it, even, because it reminds me of the life we built and shared together. And it reminds me that even if she isn't here anymore, I can help to keep her around by telling her stories and remembering the many things about her that I loved."

I find my own voice to say, "Grandpa, what if— what if she's still here? When you look for her, when you sense her presence and look for the signal— maybe it's her? What if?"

Grandpa smirks. "You're feeling superstitious today, kiddo. First you got all excited about the owls, and now you're thinking that your grandma's ghost might be hanging around?" He chuckles and shrugs and tells me, "Hey. I'm just one guy. I won't pretend to know what's real or not real. If you think she's here, watching over us—sure, why not? As I told you earlier, it's up to you to decide your own beliefs, Wesley."

"I think it could be real. I think she might still be here." I feel my shoulder blades pinch together as I ask, "Don't you agree? Possibly? Maybe?"

"Maybe," he allows. "Just maybe."

32

Uncle Kenji comes home next. His work folder is tucked awkwardly under one armpit, and his car keys jingle in his hand. He's wearing a T-shirt with a colorful graphic of the periodic table on it, followed by the words *I wear this T-shirt periodically*.

"Hey, guys," Kenji says. He glances at the TV. "Still watching this?"

"She's a talented young woman, Kenji," Grandpa barks defensively. "I'd like to see *you* take on five zombies at once, with nothing but a broom!"

Kenji's dark brows nearly hit his hairline. "Okay, then." And with that, he mutters some excuse about work emails and hurries up the stairs.

Then Auntie Jess and Baby Zoe come home. They're wearing matching, knotted head scarves, and cream-colored sundresses with ruffles on their sleeves and skirts. Auntie also has a stack of dentalium shell bracelets on her wrist, plus dentalium shell drop earrings. The shells are all pearly white and gently curved. Zoe's diaper bag is strapped to Auntie Jess's back, as she holds Zoe in one arm and clutches an energy drink in her free hand.

Jess greets us by saying, "I'm so glad the sun came out. We had cold rain and fog in the forecast all week, but look at this! It's an Indigenous Peoples' Day miracle."

"It's real nice," Grandpa agrees. "Real nice."

Baby Zoe beams at me, flaunting her two new teeth. I hop up and reach for her, offering to give Auntie a break. It's the best feeling in the world when Zoe reaches for me too, her smile growing even bigger. I carry her back to the couch, nuzzling her soft black hair and pressing kisses to her chipmunk cheeks. Zoe babbles and claps her hands, drool streaming freely down her chin.

"How was school today, Wes?" Auntie Jess asks, as she lifts her energy drink to her lips. Its label says *KEYED-UP LIME* in super-shiny, aggressively shouting letters.

"Um." I waver for a moment, unsure of what to say. As I trail off, I notice how Auntie Jess touches the dentalium shell bracelet on her wrist, how she spins it around and around, the same way Ryan does whenever he's lost in thought. It makes my heart pinch.

"It was fine," I finally manage to say, though I don't think I fool anybody. Auntie Jess tilts her head, her brown eyes softening with concern. And Grandpa actually looks away from the TV, even though he has been surprisingly invested in the house-building game that Gemma is playing now. He's made many comments about her architecture and interior design choices.

I can't stand their pity, so I focus on Baby Zoe, who is warm and wriggly and happy. She doesn't know anything about middle school or crushed hopes yet. I circle my arms around her, as she attempts to stand up on my lap, holding my shirt collar in one tiny fist. Then she loses her footing and grabs a lock of my hair to hold herself steady. I wince and hiss through my teeth.

Auntie Jess sets her drink aside, rummages in the diaper bag for a moment, and whisks out a chocolate bar from one of its pockets. "Here," she offers, extending the chocolate to me. "I'll trade you. I bet that baby needs a diaper change, and I'm sure Kenji wants to see her."

I gratefully accept the chocolate. Auntie lifts Zoe in her arms, hugging her close as she takes her away up the stairs.

As I'm finishing my chocolate bar, my mother's car pulls into the driveway. Vader magically reappears on the windowsill, purring as he waits for her. He hunkers down on the ledge, peering through the glass. The Jeep's engine shuts off, but Mom doesn't emerge right away. The sunshine glare on her windshield makes it impossible to see what she's doing.

Eventually, her door pops open. She climbs out, moving slowly, sluggishly. Her cherry cola hair is pulled back in a messy ponytail, and she has two overflowing bags of groceries in her arms.

Grandpa notices her too, and he jumps up—his knee popping audibly—to open the front door for her.

Her voice is soft and tired sounding as she steps inside and says, "Thanks, Dad."

He takes a bag of groceries from her and murmurs, "I've got this. I've got you, kiddo."

Grandpa leads her through the living room

toward the kitchen, and Mom flashes a smile my way that doesn't quite touch her eyes. "Wesley, love. How are you? How was school?"

"It was great, Mom." I make myself sound more enthusiastic than I feel, for her sake.

"Good, good."

She follows Grandpa into the kitchen. They put the groceries away together, speaking in low tones that I can't hear over the audio of Gemma's channel. Vader circles Mom's feet, brushing up against her, curling his tail so it winds around her calves.

33

At one point in their conversation, Grandpa gives a brisk shake of his head and unleashes a colorful string of curse words. Mom stops and shoots him a look, nodding in my direction.

But Grandpa keeps going.

"Pumpkin," he says, his voice rising with his frustration, "you need to find another salon. Rent a chair someplace where they'll actually appreciate you."

"It's not that simple, Dad—"

"Or better yet, start your *own* business. Work for yourself, and no one else."

"I'm not having this conversation again right now."

"I think you should. I think it's time. I can help you with the financing—"

"Dad. I'm doing the work, and I'm setting money aside, but it's just not going to happen anytime soon for me. Wesley's future comes first. It has to."

Grandpa hangs his head. Pinches the bridge of his nose between two fingers. "There is still plenty of time to save money for Wesley's college education. And as I've said, I can help with that, too."

"Have you seen tuition rates lately? Even with help from *both* of us, she might need to take out loans. She might . . ." Mom trails off, rolling her shoulders back. "Doesn't matter. The point is, I have my reputation and my clients, and there's a competition clause in my contract. I can't afford to start over in a new place. It is what it is, and it's not a big deal. I'm fine."

"Cadence."

"I'm *fine.*"

Mom shuts the cabinet door. Crumples the plastic bag in her hands. Vader meows and purrs and presses his face against her leg. Grandpa gives another small shake of his head and turns away, stacking cereal boxes on top of the refrigerator.

In the sudden silence between them, Gemma and her guest burst out laughing, the volume too loud.

Mom clears her throat. She comes back to the living room, smiling at me again, a smile that is actively trying too hard to be cheerful. She joins me on the couch and scoots in close, pulling my legs across her lap as she leans in to kiss my hair, my cheek.

She says, "Tell me about your day."

"It was great," I say again, except this time the words come out hollow sounding.

"Yeah?" A small crease forms between her brows. Her brown eyes scan my face.

I don't know what she sees when she looks at me, exactly. But whatever it is, it must be close to the truth, because her lips press together in a firm line. "Ah. Wesley, love." She pulls me even closer to her, hugging me and settling her chin against the top of my head. It makes me feel like a little kid again, when she holds me like this. "Tomorrow is a new day," she tells me gently. "Tomorrow will be better."

I breathe in deep, inhaling her familiar scent. Her clothes smell like the salon—like burned hair and hairspray. But somewhere beneath that distinct chemical aroma and the bright pop of her peppermint chewing gum, I catch a whiff of her skin. Clean and warm and impossible to name. It's just her. My mother.

Across the room, Grandpa gathers his wallet and keys and mutters about some vague errand he needs to run. He kicks his feet into his shoes and trudges out the front door.

Mom peeks out the window. She sighs as his old station wagon reverses out of the driveway.

"Is everything okay, Mom?"

"Everything's fine, love. It's all good." She leans away from me, sitting upright on the couch. "How about we turn Gemma off, and you go do your homework and practice your viola? We have the powwow at Coastline tonight. Probably won't have time to do it later; I'm sure we'll be home pretty late."

"Yeah. Sure."

I turn off the TV, grab my backpack, and make my way upstairs to work in our bedroom. Along the way, I glance at my mother. She stretches out on the couch and closes her eyes. Vader hops up into her lap, and she places her hand on his head, scratching him behind the ears.

34

This might sound strange, but when I was little—really little, preschool age—I thought that I didn't have a dad. I'd never met him, and I was too young to understand how families came to be, how babies entered the world. I was wise enough to know that lots of kids had two parents. Almost every TV show that I watched had families with a mom and dad. And I met plenty of kids who came from families like that—at the park, in swim lessons, at summer day camps. But there seemed to be just as many kids whose families were more like mine, with various arrangements of adults and guardians.

Eventually, in early elementary school, I learned the truth. I learned that my mother was a single parent and that I had a father out there somewhere. And I confronted Mom, demanding to know if this was true, and she confirmed it. She told me his name was Chris. She said that he wasn't around because he chose not to be, and she insisted that it was *his* loss, not ours. Because I was the greatest thing to ever come into either of their lives, and if he couldn't see that, it was his own fault.

Which was a good enough explanation for me. I agreed with my mother. I didn't miss him, that man named Chris who didn't go to the hospital on the day I was born, and who hadn't shown up for me ever since. I knew my mother would never abandon me. I knew who my family was.

Then when I was ten years old, Chris had a change of heart.

My mother told me about it. She said that Chris had reached out to her online, asking to reconnect, asking for the chance to meet me. She broke the news as she often did, over cups of hot cocoa out on the balcony of our old apartment. I remember the worried look in her eyes as she watched my reaction, a feather of steam curling from the mug clutched in her hands.

"Wesley, love. I want this to be entirely your choice. Do you want to meet him?"

I decided that I was curious enough to say yes.

We met Chris for lunch at a Mexican restaurant. Mom and I arrived at noon and were seated at a window booth. He was running late, so we sat there eating from the warm basket of tortilla chips, dipping each golden triangle into the small bowls of salsa and pico de gallo. The laminated menus gleamed on the table, mariachi band music played merrily in the background, and beads of condensation dripped down the sides of our water glasses.

Finally, he came. Mom had only shown me a few pictures of him, but most of them were distorted or hazy-looking or color-tinted, due to the filters he'd used in his social media posts. It was strange, to see him so clearly for the first time. He was Mom's age: twenty-seven years old. He had wavy, sand-colored hair that was nearly grown out to his shoulders, dark brown eyes, and thick eyebrows that came together to form a straight line. He wore patchy jeans, a brown leather jacket, a sturdy pair of boots. His footsteps *clop-clopped* in a heavy rhythm as he approached our table.

At first glance, he and I didn't look too much alike. I have my mother's naturally straight, dark hair, her bright brown eyes, and her thin, short frame.

But when he reached us and stood at the edge of our table, I looked up into his face and saw a lot of myself there, too. I had inherited his nose, his mouth, the dimple in his chin. My skin wasn't quite as light as his, nor was it as tan as my mother's. My brows were also on the thicker side, and now I knew why.

For a long moment, Chris stood there and said nothing. Then softly, he said, "Wow. She really is beautiful, isn't she?"

My knee-jerk reaction was to say, "Thank you."

My mother, on the other hand, stared stonily at him with her arms crossed over her chest.

"She's the spitting image of you, Cadence," Chris told her. "I like what you've done with your hair, by the way. The dark red is nice."

I sat up a little straighter and smiled at Mom, expecting the mood to lighten. But his compliments had no effect on her at all.

When she spoke, her voice resembled a darkening sky, a gathering stormfront: "Our server took our orders a few minutes ago. You should sit and decide what you want, if you do plan to join us."

I had never, ever heard that tone from my mother before. It chilled me to my core.

But Chris seemed unsurprised. He nodded and mumbled an apology, then scooted into the seat across from us, his gaze dropping to study the menu.

35

My mother is an incredibly warm and friendly and forgiving person. I don't think she has ever been truly angry with me. Not even when I was teeny-tiny, throwing tantrums in grocery stores. Not even that one day in the second grade, when I was sent to the principal's office for pushing a kid on the playground, after they kept making fun of Hanan's mother's accent.

The few times I had ever seen her angry, it was really more like frustration, or stress. Something temporary and not too serious.

But she was angry with Chris. I could tell. I

could feel it radiating from her, ice cold and scalding at the same time.

He would say something sheepish and apologetic like, "Sorry again for being late; you know, the traffic was crazy."

And she would respond with a clipped: "Well. It's been ten years. What's another twenty minutes, right?"

Then he asked me questions about myself, about my hobbies, or the things that I liked. And as I told him about my favorite video games, he grinned and said: "A gamer! You must have gotten that from me." And Mom nearly choked on her water, clearing her throat with an exaggerated cough, a loud thump of her fist against the center of her chest.

By the end of the meal, Chris groaned and said, "I'm trying here, okay? Can't you see that I'm trying, Cadence?"

"I can see that you think you are."

"What does that even mean?"

Mom ignored him. Instead, she waved our server down to ask for the checks, then focused intently on removing her debit card from her wallet, *tap-tap-tapping* it against the table.

"Why can't you tell me what you're thinking?" Chris snapped at her. "I hate it when you do this.

You do it all the time. You just expect me to know what I'm doing wrong, but I'm not a mind reader. I don't know what you want from me!"

"At the moment, all I want is to pay for my food and get my girl home. She's got homework due tomorrow."

"Okay. Well. This was fun, right? We've had a good time catching up, haven't we?"

Mom made a noncommittal noise.

Chris pressed on, determined. "Although, I do wish we would have spent more time talking about you, Cadence. You barely post anything online anymore, and you haven't said much tonight. Which was okay," he added with a quick smile at me. "Because of course, the whole purpose of this dinner was for me to get to know Wesley better."

He paused, waiting for a reaction from Mom; she didn't give him anything.

"But maybe we can get together again soon?" he said. "The three of us. Or if it's okay with you, Cadence, just the two of us?"

Her responding glare across the table made *me* wince. I had no idea how Chris managed to weather it, still with a hopeful look on his face.

"Christopher," Mom said. "Don't."

"Come on," he pleaded. "Give me a chance."

"I need you to stop talking. Right now."

"You're being stubborn for no reason. I've apol-
ogized for everything; I'm here, trying to bury the
hatchet so we can move forward, and maybe even
become a proper family. Think of our daughter—"

Our server returned to our table with two
checks, and Chris immediately stopped talking,
while my mother seethed in silence. The mariachi music swelled in the background, cheery and
upbeat. I was confused and bewildered by everything Chris had said—did he want to get back
together with my mom? Was he still in love with
her? What was even happening?

As our server accepted Mom's debit card and
Chris's crumpled dollar bills, her gaze darted
among the three of us. She lingered for a moment,
blinking at Mom and me warily, like she thought
we might be in trouble.

"Is everything okay here?" she asked.

"We're fine," Chris said curtly. "Thanks."

Our server didn't waver. "Ma'am?"

Mom nodded once. "We will be. Thank you."

She didn't look convinced, but our server simply
nodded in response, and left to settle the bills.

36

Mom gripped my hand as we left the restaurant.

"Cadence! *Cadence!*"

"I'm so sorry about this, baby," Mom was saying to me, as she rushed us across the parking lot. "I'm so sorry."

I held on to my mother's hand, my adrenaline surging, my thoughts blurring. I couldn't remember the last time she'd called me "baby." I couldn't remember the last time I'd ever felt afraid of another person. But there I was. Afraid of a man. Afraid of my own father.

Something about Mom's comment to the server

set him off. Changed him completely. After our server left to process their payments, the hopeful look in his eyes faded. His face shuttered. His left hand curled into a fist on the table, his knuckles white and taut as he stared us down.

"You will be?" he asked rigidly. "What does that mean? You *will* be."

"Chris, please—"

"That you'll be fine once I'm gone, right? Once you leave with my daughter. Once you walk away from the possibility of us being a family all over again—"

"The daughter you've ignored for ten years, Chris. Ten years! You have no right to her, or to accuse me of taking her away from you, when this separation was your choice from the very beginning."

He roared, "*My* choice?"

As Mom went on, "It's a choice you made when you walked out on me while I was pregnant, and it's a choice you made over and over with every missed milestone, every skipped birthday, every single *precious* day of her life. You never changed her diapers. You never held her or rocked her to sleep or cooked meals for her. You didn't cry during her first days of school. You didn't take her to music camps or swim lessons. You didn't teach her how to pitch a tent in the woods, or how to build a camp-fire to keep herself warm."

"I get it; I've been gone, I know! And by the way, does she even know why I've been gone? The fight we had before she was born?"

"Oh, I'm sorry, are you referring to the fight that happened over a decade ago, which you *specifically* mentioned in your text to me, claiming that you wanted a fresh start?"

That was it. The final straw.

His compliments and good manners were gone. His fist slammed down, rattling the plates and glasses on our table. His chest heaved; his eyes bulged. He unleashed a string of harsh, angry words, cursing at my mother and insulting her. He insulted her looks, her intelligence, her job as a hairdresser, her abilities as a mother, her entire family. He used slurs I had never even heard in the real world before. Slurs that I knew existed, words that I'd been told never to repeat or listen to, and now here they were, being flung at us from across our dinner table. From the mouth of my own biological father.

He was like a mad, spitting cat. Snarling and raging and vengeful.

"Sir—*sir*! Sir, I must ask you to leave, right now," our server practically shouted, as she came running back to our table. She set the checks down. Looked at Mom. "Ma'am, are you okay?"

Mom had her wallet again. She slipped a few bills out, took her card back from the server, and handed her the tip. Then she grabbed my hand and strode out of the restaurant, the peppy mariachi music growing louder as we approached the door, and as Chris came hurrying after us, ignoring the attempts of restaurant staff and onlookers to intervene.

We burst through the glass doors. We ran across the parking lot.

"Cadence! *Cadence!*"

Mom used her key fob to unlock the Jeep. "Quickly, Wesley," she urged, releasing my hand. "*Quickly.*"

I dashed around to the passenger side and hopped up into the car, fumbling with my seat belt buckle as Mom's foot slammed the brake. She started the ignition, locked the doors.

Chris threw himself against Mom's door, his face pressed to the windowpane. He had seemed normal before, handsome even, but his face was all twisted now. Ravaged by a sudden, severe sadness. His dark eyes shone with tears as he wailed my mother's name.

"I'm sorry," he begged. "I'm sorry, but you know

this, *you know* I've never stopped loving you. After all these years, I've never stopped, and I never will! It hurts me so badly every time you try to leave me, Cadence. I'm sorry I yelled, but you know the effect you have on me. You make me feel crazy. It's only because I care. I care so, so much—"

Mom revved the engine. "Let us *go*," she shouted through the closed glass.

"You're breaking my heart," Chris whined. "Think of our daughter. She needs me. She needs her father."

Mom shifted into reverse, checked over her shoulder, and shot out of the space, leaving Chris bewildered, shouting about how she'd nearly crushed his toes. Mom didn't linger. The Jeep set off through the parking lot with a roar, blasting past stop signs like they didn't even exist. We swerved into the stream of traffic down the main road, and Mom pulled farther and farther ahead, accelerating and weaving between cars.

The silence between us was tense. I watched as her hands gripped the wheel, as she fought back against the tears sliding down her cheeks with clenched teeth.

I had no idea what to do.

37

That night, after I had finished my homework packet and brushed my teeth and changed into my pajamas, I tiptoed down the hallway of our apartment to check on my mother. I still felt alert and a little jumpy, after our rushed exit from the restaurant. I couldn't imagine what she must have been going through.

Mom was sprawled on the couch in our living room, her dark red hair fanned across the throw pillows, her gaze focused on the television. She was rewatching *Star Wars: Episode III—Revenge of the Sith*, probably for the thousandth time. Vader was curled up in her lap with his eyes closed, his nose tucked inside the curve of his tail. The curtains were open, and the sky outside was a deep, starless indigo. Cars sped down the freeway lanes, endless strobes of bright whites and glowing red taillights.

I hovered at the edge of the room.

Mom broke the silence first by saying, "Come, join me."

She opened her arms to me, and I nestled in, doing my best not to bother the cat. But even though he normally liked to have Mom all to himself, Vader reached out with one arm, purring as he pressed his paw against my leg. Mom pulled me closer, so the top of my head was fitted perfectly beneath her chin.

"This is my comfort movie," she murmured. "I have no idea how many times I've watched it."

"Same," I said. "Padmé is my favorite character."

Mom nodded in agreement. "She's the most underrated character in the galaxy far, far away. I love her."

We focused on the action for a bit. The buzzing clash of lightsabers, the choreography of the fight scenes, the iconic lines of dialogue.

After a while, Mom cleared her throat and said, "When I was younger, I had the biggest crush on Anakin. I thought it was so romantic, how he was willing to do anything to keep Padmé safe. How he even went to the Dark Side for her." She nuzzled the top of my head. Her arm around me tightened. "I was wrong, of course. There's nothing romantic about his anger, his insecurity, his mood swings. He didn't go to the Dark Side for love; he went for the power."

It felt like we weren't talking about *Star Wars* anymore. I placed my hand over Mom's.

"Padmé deserved better," I said. "She deserved someone good. Someone brave enough to stay in the light for her."

"I agree. I agree."

It was getting late. The sky outside darkened further. I felt warm and safe and content in my mother's arms. My eyelids were heavy, drooping.

"You're a bit young for romance," Mom whispered to me, her voice hoarse with emotion. "But when that time comes, promise me you won't ever settle for an Anakin. Promise you will only accept the love that you deserve."

I blinked slowly. "I promise, Mom."

Her breathing turned ragged. She grasped my shoulder, and I noticed her hand was trembling.

She kept holding me close as I drifted to sleep.

We haven't seen Chris at all since that day. And I haven't missed him one bit.

38

By the time I finish my homework and go downstairs, Grandpa has returned from his errands, Mom has disappeared to take a shower, Auntie Jess and Uncle Kenji are playing with Zoe on the rug in the living room, and Vader has curled up on the windowsill.

It's a typical Monday afternoon.

"What time are we going to Coastline?" Auntie Jess groans. "I'm starving."

Grandpa says, "Once Cadence is ready, we'll go. The food vendors should be all set up by now."

Every year on Indigenous Peoples' Day, we

attend a public intertribal powwow that takes place in the gym at Coastline High School. It's the only one we regularly go to. There are plenty of Native families who tour the entire continent by traveling around to different powwows. Some of them go to perform and compete in the dance contests; others go to sell their food or T-shirts or crafts and jewelry. Some of them go to spectate and socialize and spend time with their friends and family. People gather at powwows for countless reasons—that's one thing that makes them so special. Folks come from anywhere and everywhere, to celebrate and to share and to show their pride in the Native community.

"Can I check my *Spacefaring Wanderers* account?" I ask. "I want to send Hanan a message so she knows she can start the next quest without me tonight."

"Sure," Grandpa says. "But then you need to put that Gemma girl back on after you're done."

I agree to his terms and turn on the game console. I grab my controller, navigate to the main menu, and open my inbox. There are two unread messages, and I expect them both to be from Hanan, but they're not. The first is a friend request from ella_holland. The second is a note from her that says: *hi again, this is ella! i cant stay online because i have a tutoring session tonight, but wanted to say hi ☺ maybe we can play tomorrow? ive been stuck on this one gem quest on the ice planet FOREVER.*

You need to partner with friends on the ice planet. You just need to. Those puzzles are way too hard to unlock alone, unless you have a huge stock of power-ups. Even then, they can be tricky.

I type out a response to Ella, then I send my message to Hanan, along with a link to Ella's account so she can send her a friend request. Between the three of us, those ice planet gems won't stand a chance.

With that all sorted, I turn the console off and return to gemmakitty01's livestream.

As Grandpa continues to watch the stream, I join my baby cousin on the floor, causing Zoe to squeal with delight. Wooden blocks engraved with letters from the alphabet are scattered all around her, and I start to gather them up, stacking them in towers for her to knock over. It's a simple game: I count the letters, spell simple words, and each time a stack builds to three or four blocks, Zoe swipes at them, sending them tumbling across the floor.

Zoe giggles heartily as we play. Her beautiful, dark eyes twinkle with mischief. And I keep building new words for her, mostly out of the same handful of letters, words like *TOO* and *TOP* and *STOP*. She bats them apart and laughs as they fall. Auntie Jess and Uncle Kenji and I laugh along with her.

Eventually, Uncle Kenji says, "I want to buy her more block games like these, except with Japanese characters and symbols."

I perk up. "Wait, you know Japanese? Are you fluent?"

Uncle Kenji shrugs, embarrassed. "Definitely not fluent. I can follow along when my parents speak in Japanese, but I have a hard time forming sentences myself. It's something I want to become better at, though. And I want Zoe to learn it, too."

"That would be cool," I agree. "I wish I knew other languages. I really want to take French and Spanish electives in school, but I'll have to either choose one or drop orchestra next year. I'm not sure what to do yet."

Grandpa's voice sounds gravelly and somber again as he says, "I wish I knew how to speak Lushootseed."

A sort of sad, contemplative silence falls over us. Aside from Baby Zoe, who is happily shaking a lion-shaped rattle, our game with the alphabet blocks forgotten. And also the chirpy video game tones and overlapping conversation from gemma-kitty01's livestream.

Grandpa says, "Lushootseed was the primary language of our family for generations, for who knows how long. It's how our people's stories were shared. It's how the knowledge was passed down. And then came the boarding schools, the English-only rules, the English-only American society." He glances at Uncle Kenji and says, "Get those Japanese alphabet blocks for Zoe. Make sure she learns the language. Make sure she understands what a gift it is."

39

Mom comes downstairs a few minutes later. She looks refreshed and happy. She has showered and blow-dried and styled her hair in long, soft waves. Ever since I was little, we've always called this style her "mermaid hair."

I perk up and tell her, "Nice mermaid hair, Mom!"

Auntie Jess chimes in with, "Yeah, Cadence, you look great."

She really does. Her outfit is simple: she's wearing burgundy Converse All-Stars, black leggings, and a plum-and-black plaid flannel. Her skin is dewy from her moisturizer, and she has put on a purplish lip color and black mascara, the final touches to bring her casual but pretty look together.

"Thanks," Mom says, a little bashfully. "I'm feeling pretty great. Are we ready to head out?"

We are. Grandpa turns the TV off; at this point, Gemma has raised over twenty thousand dollars, which is so much money, it blows my mind. Auntie Jess and Uncle Kenji run through a quick diaper bag checklist, to make sure Baby Zoe is all set for our outing. Vader slinks over to Mom and presses his cheek against her shin.

And then we all file out the door, Grandpa locking up behind us. Jess and Kenji and Zoe go into Kenji's black sedan; Grandpa and Mom and I climb into Mom's green Jeep.

Once the three of us are alone, Grandpa clears his throat and says, "Cadence . . ." And it occurs to me that they haven't spoken since their argument.

I watch from the back seat as Grandpa turns to her. Sunlight slants through the car windows, starkly illuminating the wrinkles along his tanned skin, the light-brown color of his irises.

Mom meets his gaze. Her cherry cola hair glows purplish and red in the sun. Her profile is a younger, softer mirror image of Grandpa's: the same brown eyes, the same straight nose.

Her voice is soft as she says, "It's okay, Dad."

"I only want what's best for you. That's why I brought the salon thing up again, that's why I keep asking—"

"I know you do. You don't have to explain. It really is okay."

His shoulders slump. "I just wish things were easier for you."

Mom reaches over to pat his knee. "You worry too much. I have a lot to be grateful for. I have you; I have Wesley. I get to raise my daughter in the same house that I grew up in. How many people can say that? How many people are able to stay where their family's roots are? It's so rare," she says. "It's such a difficult thing to do in this constantly changing, competitive, uncertain world. A lot of folks get forced out. A lot of people lack support systems or places to go."

"Not you," Grandpa says earnestly.

"Not me," Mom agrees. "I'm very lucky. Very grateful."

She shifts gears and reverses the Jeep easily out of the driveway. We follow Kenji's black sedan down to the end of our cul-de-sac. I roll my window down as we approach the woods that border the street. Golden sunlight slants through the trees, dappling the ground in shifting bright spots and shadows.

"You and Wesley can stay with me forever, for all I care," Grandpa says. "Same goes for your sister and her family."

Mom gives a breathy laugh. "Well. I'm not going anywhere anytime soon. We'll see if Jess and Kenji stick around, too."

I lean forward fast, jolting my seat belt as I ask, "Why *wouldn't* they stick around?"

"They might move," Mom tells me. "Kenji was offered a job in Tennessee. A friend of his is a principal down there, and they're really suffering from the teacher shortage. He and Jess are still talking it over, but they're definitely considering it. I know she would be happy to leave the current hospital. She's getting so burned out there."

This is the first I'm hearing of this. I stare straight through the windshield; Baby Zoe is buckled into her backward-facing car seat in Uncle Kenji's car, so I can see her from here. She is gnawing on a plastic teething ring, kicking her little feet so contentedly.

"Tennessee?" I repeat weakly. In my mind, I try to picture a map of the US. I'm not sure where

Tennessee is exactly, but I know it's somewhere in the Southeast, whereas we are in the Northwest.

Baby Zoe would be so far away from me.

How often would they come home? Would we ever go visit them? Would Zoe grow up speaking with a Southern accent? Would she remember me? Would she know me?

Mom sighs as we pull out of the cul-de-sac, following Uncle Kenji's car onto the main road. "I'm sorry, love," she tells me. "That wasn't how I wanted to break the news; nothing is set in stone, okay? It's possible they might stay. They might not go anywhere."

I nod, even as a lump forms in the base of my throat.

I know what Mom really means when she says things like: *It's possible they might stay.* The truth is probably closer to: *It's only a matter of time before they go.*

40

As we continue on our way to Coastline High School, the road slopes down, down, down. The traffic crawls slower and slower as we approach the beach at the bottom of a steep bluff.

Then, finally, the road leads us into a freshly paved parking lot. It's a sprawling, wide-open space between the high school and the shimmering blue waters of the Puget Sound. The Olympic Peninsula and Olympic Mountains rise across the western horizon, on the opposite side of the Sound. Whidbey, Camano, and Gedney Islands are all green and forested and beautiful in the rippling water. The

Tulalip Bay curves around the sparkling waters to the north, and the delta of the Snohomish River opens wide to the east. The parking lot's rows and rows are packed with all kinds of cars and trucks and vans. I notice bumper stickers that range from clear expressions of Native pride to silly or morbidly funny jokes to college alumni affiliations. I see license plates from British Columbia and California and North Carolina and Oklahoma.

Mom and Kenji find two spots at the far end of the lot. We all climb out of the cars, and I can't help but linger to watch as Auntie Jess unbuckles Baby Zoe. Jess hoists Zoe onto her hip, and Zoe giggles and sticks her tiny fist into her mouth, and I resist the urge to press kisses all over her chubby, perfect little cheeks.

Eight months old today. It feels like forever, and also like barely any time has passed at all. It feels like I've known her my entire life, and also like she just got here.

She's the little sister I've never had. The baby cousin who made me nervous, when Mom and I first planned to move in with Grandpa. It's weird to look back on that now, to remember how I fretted over the possibility of sleepless nights, or the prospect of sharing one-point-five bathrooms between too many people.

Now—if this happens, if they really do leave—I'm afraid that the house might feel too big without them. That it might feel empty. And different.

I follow my family to the school's entrance. Along the way, we pass by groups of fancy dancers in their full regalia. Women pulling wagons piled high with folded, brightly patterned blankets. A man with a pierced eyebrow, who insists on handing Mom one of his burned CDs; he autographs the plain silver disk with a black Sharpie, his signature impossible to read. We hear deep belly laughs, the *tink-tink-tink* of jingle dresses, the rise and fall of a rogue wave across the shoreline. A tiny tot in a pink jingle dress tugs at her mother's skirt and points at Zoe, shouting, "Look! Look, there's a baby! Hi, baby!"

As we step up onto the sidewalk, Mom wraps one arm around my shoulders. She gives me a squeeze as she asks, "You okay, Wesley?"

I take a moment to hold her question in my heart. Am I okay? I don't really know. What a sad, strange day this has been. And I'd had such high hopes for it.

I think about my poem, unread and discarded by so many of my classmates.

I think about Ryan, wearing another girl's Tolo bracelet.

I think about my extended family, possibly moving on to live under separate roofs again.

Mom hugs me against her side, waiting.

And I decide to tell her, "I will be."

Even though I'm unhappy right now. Even though this day didn't go according to plan. I tell her I will be okay, because I need those words to be true.

I need to believe it myself.

41

Coastline High School is massive and modern. We cross the wide terrace and follow the arrow signs that guide us around the main office building and to the gymnasium, where the powwow is being held. A row of vendors line the sidewalk. Some of their booths are stocked with handmade wares and jewelry; others offer sign-up sheets for free health screenings, voter registration cards, and information on various social services. The doors to the gym have been propped open. The crowd thickens as we grow closer, and before we even step inside the building, I can hear the thrumming rhythm of the drum circle.

We've made it just in time for the Grand Entry.

We step inside the building, into a hallway lined with cinder blocks, trophy cases, team photos and pennant flags and plaques that mark various athletic achievements. There are signs that point to the locker rooms and bathrooms. And there are also construction paper posters that say: *FOOD VENDORS + ARTS & CRAFTS IN CAFETERIA. THX.*

The drumming grows louder and louder the closer we get to the gym. Uncle Kenji accepts a program from a powwow volunteer and hands it to Auntie Jess. From somewhere inside the gym, the emcee's amplified voice calls out, asking the dancers to line up for the Grand Entry.

"Should we watch them come in first, then go get food?" Auntie Jess asks.

"Sounds good," Mom agrees.

I follow my family into the gym. The bleachers are long and wide across the expanse, and they're filling up fast with spectators and draped blankets. The emcee's command center and the drum circle are all arranged beneath the basketball hoop on the opposite side of the room. The gym floor is open, its rows of tawny-golden planks gleaming brightly, with a giant capital *C* in the middle of the space.

"Mac! Mac Wilder, over here!"

A group of men about Grandpa's age wave at us and motion him over. One of them is wearing a US Navy veteran cap. Another has sleeves of black-gray tattoos all over his arms and neck. The third is wearing aviator sunglasses, even though we're indoors.

"Ha!" Grandpa pops his flannel's collar and points at the *ELDERS ONLY* signs that are taped to the bottom two rows of bleachers, where the men are now moving aside for him. "VIP seating," he says coolly. "Looks like the rest of you are on your own. See ya later."

He strides off to join his friends, while we laugh and shake our heads and climb higher in search of an open space.

The Grand Entry is my favorite part of the powwow. (Aside from the food, of course.) There's just something about how traditional it feels, how the entire community rises and comes together to witness the dancers as they gather in an ever-tightening circle. It feels big and important. Like we are a part of something truly significant.

I'm standing on the bleachers between Mom and Uncle Kenji, who is now holding Zoe in a baby carrier strapped to his chest. Everyone else around us is standing too, as the emcee announces the names of the veterans who are carrying the military service flags and leading the parade of dancers into the gym. The drum circle plays in a steady, upbeat rhythm; the men's voices rise and warble in unison. The dancers continue to file in, in the order of their category appearances, with numbers pinned to their regalia. Men enter the circle bobbing and swaying, hopping on their feet, flashing their colorful feather bustles. Women follow in their musical jingle dresses and patterned shawls. I can see smiles and looks of deep concentration on their faces as they step and hop and bounce through their footwork.

The teens come next. I recognize the Coastline High School colors in one boy's regalia. One of the girls is carrying her cheer poms, shimmying them proudly as the jingles in her dress go *tink-tink-tink!* The junior boys and girls are next, following closely behind the teenagers, and there is a girl among them who catches my eye. Whose presence nearly makes me gasp. The tiny tots are making their way into the gym now, capturing the attention of everyone in the audience with their cuteness, but I can't look away from her.

From the girl in the electric blue dress, adorned with jingling silver cones.

From the girl whose auburn hair has been styled into two neat braids that frame her face.

From the girl who is new to my school, and who arrived late to our science class today.

Skye Reynolds is here. And she's dancing in the powwow.

42

I find Skye in the crowd again an hour later, just as I'm finishing up my bowl of corn soup and my plate of fry bread. I'm seated at a table in the middle of the cafeteria with my mom, who is chatting with a woman who teaches a language workshop at a local heritage center. And Skye is standing in line for a snow cone. She is alone and staring intently at her phone.

I tap my mother's arm and say, "Hey, Mom, I'm done eating. Do you mind if I go say hi to my friend over there?"

"Go ahead," she says distractedly. "We're heading back to the gym soon. You know where to find me."

I give her a quick, one-armed hug and hop up out of my seat. I take my used utensils and dirty napkin to the compost bin, then make my way across the room to Skye. I have no idea what to say to her. We didn't exactly talk much when we became lab partners today.

But I think I want to get to know her. So I'm just going to figure it out.

She looks so different in her powwow regalia. I can't help but compare the image of her now to the image in my memory from this morning: The oversized, faded green T-shirt versus the electric shades of blue. The shiny black leggings versus the glinting silver cones. Her face has been washed clean, and her braids have been redone and laced with sky-colored ribbons.

Her gaze is still focused on her glowing phone screen as I clear my throat and say, "Um. Hey. Hi."

Skye blinks up at me. Her mouth pops open with surprise. "Oh, whoa. Hey, Wesley."

"Hey." We stare at each other for a second; I gesture at her jingle dress. "I had no idea," I tell her.

"You look great, by the way. Really cool."

She blushes. "Thank you. My mother made me this dress." She looks down at herself and shifts from side to side, letting the jingle cones sway and clink. Then she looks at me again, and asks, "Do you want some shaved ice?"

"I don't have any money . . ." I rise onto my tiptoes and glance back, but Mom is no longer seated at the same table.

"That's okay," Skye says quickly. "My treat."

"Really? Are you sure?"

She smiles and holds up a wad of crumpled dollar bills in her fist.

Several minutes later, we set our cups of rainbow-syrup-drenched ice down on a table and take our seats. We each dig in with our plastic spoons, and even though I *thought* I was full after my dinner, it turns out you can always find more space in your stomach for powwow food. The chilly, sweet flakes of ice melt in my mouth. The cherry flavor is my favorite. I scoop deep into its glistening, ruby-red stripe in my bowl, savoring every bite.

And as we eat, Skye and I talk. I learn a lot about her.

I confirm that she moved here from Oklahoma

City. She grew up there, in a small redbrick house with a big green yard. She had a tree house and a tire swing in the oak tree in her backyard, and she spent her summers playing with her cousins and running through sprinklers with her siblings and the kids in her neighborhood. It sounds like she misses those experiences just as much as I miss the pool and balcony at my old apartment.

But despite how much she misses her friends and family in Oklahoma, she likes the Pacific Northwest so far. She especially loves living near the Puget Sound waterfront, and she can't wait to visit the ocean soon. Skye wants to become a marine biologist when she grows up. She loves dolphins and whales and other sea creatures. It has always been her dream to work with them and help make the oceans safer and healthier for them.

I also learn that she is a citizen of the Choctaw Nation. She has been dancing in powwows ever since she was a tiny tot, and apparently she shares tons of videos of herself dancing on her social media accounts. She unlocks her phone and shows me a feed filled with short video clips. In most of them, she's wearing her blue jingle dress, but there are plenty of other colorful dresses that belonged to her mother, her aunties, and her cousins—one is magenta pink, another is a warm shade of orange, then lemon yellow. They're all so vibrant and beautiful.

"You're lucky," I tell her. "To have family traditions like this."

She gives me a kind smile. "Tell me about it."

We scroll on together, admiring the artistry of the dresses, the music and footwork in each clip. It's some of the best online content I've ever seen.

43

Our bowls are empty, and we are both bent over Skye's phone when a familiar voice says, "Well, look at this!"

We glance around to find Ms. Gilbert and Ms. Aguilar standing behind us. Ms. Gilbert is beaming at us; she is wearing several strands of dentalium shells around her neck, and her violet-streaked hair is pulled back to reveal her matching earrings. She is also wearing a purple-and-gold Lakers T-shirt. Ms. Aguilar is wearing an intricately woven ribbon skirt and a black T-shirt with red text that says *Honor the Matriarchs*. For once, her dark hair is

down, framing her face; she looks pleasantly surprised to see us.

"I'm so happy to see you both!" Ms. Gilbert says.
"Skye, I can't wait to watch you out there with the
other junior girls."

Skye gives a bashful smile. "I won't let you
down, Ms. G." She meets my gaze and motions
between me and Ms. Gilbert. "Do you two know
each other? Ms. G, this is Wesley."

Ms. Gilbert responds with a conspiratorial
wink. "Oh, we've met. Wesley was supposed to be
in the union with us."

Skye brightens. "Really? You signed up for the
club? So did I!"

"What?" I can't help but grin. "No way."

"Yes way," Ms. Gilbert says. "This is like a mini
reunion right now. Two out of the three students
who signed up. If only Armando and Autumn were
here, too!"

We all bond for a moment over the Club That
Could Have Been. Ms. Gilbert tells us she wants to
keep trying to make the club official, and that she
and the eighth graders had spent time brainstorm-
ing ways to advertise and get the word out. Skye
and I agree to help, and we make plans to join Ms.
Gilbert in her classroom during lunch tomorrow.

"I'm looking forward to it, girls," Ms. Gilbert says, beaming. She nudges Ms. Aguilar's arm. "Anyway. I think I smell some fry bread with my name on it. Shall we, Angela?"

"Yeah. Just one second," Ms. Aguilar says. She turns her focus on Skye and tells her, "I spoke with the school principal about the incident this morning. We're going to have a staff meeting about it soon; I emailed your parents to keep everyone in the loop, and to make sure the school stays transparent and proactive moving forward. It shouldn't have happened. And, as promised, you have my full support; I'll do everything I can to make sure they're held accountable."

Color rises in Skye's cheeks again. "Thank you, Ms. Aguilar."

Ms. Aguilar gives a curt nod. "It's the least I can do."

I glance between them, remembering how upset Skye seemed when she came to class this morning. How Ms. Aguilar spoke with her after we were dismissed. How she offered her a hug once the rest of us were gone.

Ms. Gilbert gasps and snaps her fingers, as she also remembers. "Wesley! I meant to tell you—I absolutely *loved* your piece in the school newspaper today. So thoughtful and insightful. I was really impressed."

Now it's my turn to blush. "O-oh—thank you. I'm glad you liked it."

"I don't know if you heard, but the emcee is starting a new tradition tonight," Ms. Gilbert says. "He is going to give space for an open mic segment. Anyone from the community will be encouraged to share songs in their language, traditional stories, or anything like that. And I just *know* your poem would be a huge hit with the crowd. Everyone would love it."

The look on my face must be hilarious, because it makes Ms. Aguilar snort, while Ms. Gilbert cracks up laughing. I turn to Skye for support, but she only smiles and shrugs.

"No pressure or anything," Ms. Gilbert reassures me. "But please consider it."

"I, um—" I feel my cheeks burning as I grasp for an excuse. "But I don't even have a copy of the paper. With me. Right now."

Ms. Gilbert gives a semi-evil smile as she removes her purse from her shoulder and dramatically whisks a folded copy of the newspaper out of it.

"Wow," she muses. "It's almost like this little encounter was meant to be." She places the paper on the tabletop, beside my empty bowl. "I sincerely hope that I'll get to hear these words in your own voice, Wesley. Think it over; I'll see you girls at lunch tomorrow."

Both teachers stride off to get in line for food, while I stare at the newspaper in disbelief.

Ms. Gilbert's copy has been folded in a way that presents my column front and center.

Like she thought it deserved to be on the front page.

44

"Geez," Skye says, once the teachers are out of earshot. "That must be a great poem. She teaches honors English for the eighth graders, you know."

I did know that. I can't stop staring at the copy of the newspaper she left for me.

Mr. Holt thought that my words didn't deserve extra credit; Ms. Gilbert thinks they're worthy of an open mic.

How strange.

I meet Skye's gaze again. I want to ask about what happened before she came to science class. What Ms. Aguilar was talking about. But I'm not sure how. I don't know where to begin.

Skye's blue eyes soften. She stares back at me with a smile that looks sad around the edges.

Then she takes her phone. Opens her camera roll. Turns the phone to face me and says, "This is how I came to school this morning."

My breath catches. This picture looks nothing like the Skye I saw earlier. I recognize the red and black ribbons woven into her braids. The shiny black leggings and heavy black combat boots.

But the shirt is different. Instead of an over-sized and faded green shirt, she is wearing a fitted black T-shirt printed with these words: *Columbus Never "Discovered" US*.

Her face is also different. The lower half of her face has been painted with the shape of a red handprint. Its palm covers her mouth and chin. Its fingers extend across her cheeks.

"It's true, you know," Skye says. Her voice is so soft, so timid at first. But when I meet her gaze, she lifts her chin and continues with more confidence. "Columbus didn't discover the Americas. North America was never a 'New World'; this continent is just as old as Europe, just as old as every other place in the world."

I can't help but glance around. "Yeah," I agree

quietly. "I know what you mean."

"He didn't even make it here anyway," Skye declares. "That's a fact. He landed on an island in the Bahamas first and traveled around the Caribbean before he returned to Spain. He would have been one of the first Europeans in history to ever see dolphins, and so many other things, but do you know what else he wrote about? In his journals? Do you know what he reported back to Queen Isabella when he returned from that trip?"

I shake my head. I've never thought too much about Columbus, to be honest. I didn't even know that he went to the Caribbean Sea. Or that he served a Queen Isabella.

In elementary school, I remember singing a song about how "In 1492, Columbus sailed the ocean blue." That was pretty much it.

"He wrote about the Indigenous people he met and described how they would make 'fine servants.' He wrote about how they didn't recognize what his sword was, how they had no iron weapons themselves. He told his queen that he believed they could be overtaken easily. He said something like, 'With fifty men we could take them all and make them do what we want.'"

I shudder. "Really?" How have I never heard of this before?

"He was an enslaver," Skye tells me. "He was a terrible person. Which is why I always protest Columbus Day, and I always get in trouble over it. At my last school, I was suspended for calling him an enslaver in class, even though it's the *truth*. Then this morning, on my way to homeroom, a teacher stopped me in the hallway. He said my appearance was 'inappropriate,' and he sent me to the office. One of the secretaries lectured me about 'scaring my classmates,' and she made me wash my face and change into a shirt from the lost and found."

"She said you were scaring people?"

"Yes. Scaring them. That's the word she used."

"But it was only a T-shirt and some face paint."

Skye sighs. "I know. It was humiliating. They really hurt my feelings, and that shirt they gave me smelled so weird. And it didn't fit right at all."

For an embarrassingly long moment, I can't think of anything to say. My heart aches for Skye, as I imagine how lonely and awkward she must have felt all day. She's already the new girl; she already sits alone at lunch. It pains me to think about the rude adults who forced her to change her appearance. And about the rumors that have already been circulating ever since Skye came to our school.

Skye clears her throat. Meets my gaze with a brave, slightly trembly smile. "Do you mind if I read it? The poem?"

I slide the newspaper across the tabletop.

It only takes her a moment to read it. The poem is short and simple, but that's part of the reason why I had been so proud of it—because I tried to say a lot within a few quick stanzas.

Skye looks up and nods. She says, "Ms. G is right; you should read this."

Just then, two small boys in brightly colored powwow regalia come running toward us, calling out Skye's name. Judging by their reddish-brown hair and bright blue eyes, these must be her younger brothers. And it sounds like they're telling her she needs to get back to the gym now.

"The junior girls must be up next," Skye says. She smiles again and says, "This was really nice, talking with you."

"Same here. Good luck with your dancing."

"Thanks. I'll see you in science tomorrow. Then again at lunch with Ms. G!"

I tell her, "Can't wait!"

She's still smiling as she rises from her seat. She leaves to join her brothers, the jingle cones on her dress clinking with every step.

45

I return to the gym with the newspaper tucked under one arm.

As I climb the bleachers and rejoin my family, the junior girls in jingle dresses spread across the gym floor. The girls represent a wide array of Native Nations, and their dresses, their skin tones, the hair colors are all so diverse and different. Some of them smile and jump and wave at their families and supporters in the crowd; others stand tall and focused, their gazes fixed in concentration. The audience in the bleachers cheers and claps for them as the drum circle begins again, starting with a strong and steady rhythm.

I take my seat beside Mom and seek out Skye among the dancers. It's easy to pick her out of the crowd—she is one of the only redheads, and she has some of the fairest skin out of all the girls on the floor right now. And as I watch her bob and step with the rhythm of the drums, the jingle cones glinting and shimmering with every movement—I am struck again by how different she seems compared to this morning. She looks so joyful right now. So proud. Amazing.

A pang of regret throbs in my chest as I remember how standoffish I must have seemed when we first became lab partners. I could tell that she was upset from the moment she entered Ms. Aguilar's classroom. I knew that something was off. That something was wrong.

And yet—in that moment, I didn't say anything. I didn't reach out to her. I didn't try to help.

It's impossible to know what other people are going through. You never really know who might be hurting. What pain and stories they might be carrying in their hearts. But it is always possible to be kind. To be the one who might lift someone up and out of their darkest moments. To be a helper. And now, with this lesson fresh in my mind, I resolve to do the following things:

Tomorrow, I will see if Skye has a gamertag. I will invite her to play *Spacefaring Wanderers* with Hanan and Ella and me. Skye is still new to our school, and I'm not sure if she has made many friends yet; I would like to count her as a new friend, as well as my new lab partner.

Also, I am going to get serious about Ms. Gilbert's offer to join an unofficial Native/Indigenous Student Union. Even if we won't count among our school's clubs or have our own page in the yearbook—that doesn't matter to me. I want to keep meeting more Native kids in my school. I want to get involved and stay connected with our mighty little community.

And lastly, I decide that I will read my poem during the open mic tonight. I decide that I will stand tall and proud, just like the girls who are brave enough to be out there, dancing on the gym floor right now. I decide that these words I've written do matter. That I am proud of this poem. That I want it to be read and heard.

The thought of it makes me jittery and squeamish and nervous.

But I'm going to do it.

I will. I will.

46

When the emcee announces his call for an open mic and invites any interested speakers to line up on the gym floor, my mother hugs me tight and says, "I am so proud of you. You lift me up. Now go lift this entire crowd."

I feel lightheaded and fidgety as I nod, then begin my descent down the bleachers. A few people clap and shout encouragingly as I move past them, but I find I'm unable to thank them or meet their gazes. I'm too nervous and too focused on making it down these steps without my knees giving out.

Even before my feet hit the gym floor, I have

regrets. I'm contemplating turning around and running back and hiding behind my mother. The way I used to use her as a shield around strangers, when I was a small and shy little kid.

The sporadic cheers and applause continue as I shakily make my way across the shiny gym floor. I join the short line that has formed near the emcee's booth beneath the basketball hoop.

The first few speakers take their turns, but their words blur in the noise of my mind. I can't focus. My mouth feels dry. I remove the newspaper from under my arm, skim the words printed neatly in ink. The words I'm about to read in front of—so many people.

There are so many people in here.

So many.

My legs are like wobbly sticks and my fists are clammy with sweat, crumpling the edges of the newspaper as my turn comes and I step forward to approach the microphone. I'm vaguely aware of the scattered, welcoming applause. I also hear a gruff shout from somewhere nearby, and I think it might have been Grandpa's voice, but I'm not entirely sure.

But I am here.

Standing at the mic.

Staring out at the full Coastline High School gymnasium.

A sort of hush falls over the crowd, as everyone kindly waits for me to speak. In the distance, I hear a baby wailing, and the distressed pitch of the baby's cries makes me scan the crowd, wondering if it's Zoe, hoping she's okay.

And it's in this breathless moment—in this huge, crowded space—that I see him.

My world tilts.

My heart *lunges* in my chest.

Ryan. Ryan is here. Ryan Thomas is standing beside the nearest cluster of bleachers. He is wearing clean white sneakers, a pair of navy basketball shorts, and a purple *Shorelands Pride* sweatshirt. His golden-blond bangs swoop across his forehead. His eyes crinkle at the corners as he gives me a big, encouraging smile. And two thumbs-up.

It's the same smile he used to boost my confidence when we sat across the circle from each other in the first Gamer Club meeting.

The same smile I needed to see to speak up now.

I continue to hold his gaze as I lean into the mic and say, "Um. Hi. Hi, everyone, I'm Wesley. My name is Wesley Wilder, and I'm a seventh grader at Shorelands Middle School." I draw my breath. My voice is shaky, but I'm here and I'm doing it. I'm speaking. I look out across the crowd and say, "My family is Upper Skagit. I'm proud of my heritage, and I wrote this poem in honor of Indigenous Peoples' Day. It was published in the school newspaper. And now I'm going to read it to you."

That seems like enough of an introduction. It wasn't the speech I had prepared in my mind for Mr. Holt's class, when I'd hoped to share my work earlier, but it will do. I'll let my words speak for themselves.

I inhale deeply, and recite my poem:

We belong to the rushing rivers, the
life-giving lakes, the seas, the oceans.
We belong to the forests, the deserts, the
prairies, the mountains.
We belong to the skyscraper cities, the
neighborly suburbs, the wide-open country.
We belong to the ancient past, the here and
now, the futures that are coming.
We belong to this world, these Nations, our
families.

They might try to force us from these places.
They might forget us in their stats and
stories.
They might claim that we don't count.
They might pretend we don't exist.

But no matter what games they play,
always remember this:
We still belong.
We still belong.
We still belong.

47

My face is on fire, my heart is hammering in my chest, and I'm so happy and relieved and glad that I worked up the courage to present my poem here. The responding applause moves and feels like thunder. I duck my head and retreat to the gym's sidelines as if I'm escaping from a storm.

And Ryan is still there. Smiling and clapping and holding eye contact as I cross the space to him.

Grandpa's words from earlier echo in my mind: *That was it. The signal.*

The applause dies down as I reach the edge of the bleachers, but Ryan keeps on clapping, even as the distance between us closes.

Every time our eyes met, I felt like I was exactly where I was supposed to be. Every time I found her in a crowd, it was like coming home.

Ryan and I are standing face-to-face. His hands are still moving, still clapping, almost automatically. The gym has mostly returned to silence in anticipation of the next speaker, and I watch as Ryan seems to realize this, his own applause trailing off as he awkwardly fumbles his fingertips and starts to play with the *EVILO* bracelet on his wrist, twisting it and tugging at its purple strand.

I can't help but notice the fact that he isn't wearing his *TOLO* bracelet.

I can't help but think that he looks nervous.

He sounds breathless as he says, "Hi. Good job. That was—that was really good."

"Thanks," I say, and I sound just as bewildered as I feel. "How are you—what are you doing here?"

"I, um—" His green eyes flick over my shoulder, focusing on the next presenter as they start to speak. Then he lowers his voice to ask, "Do you wanna go find someplace better to talk?"

"Sure. Let me just . . ." I glance beyond him, scanning the area of the bleachers where Mom is seated. She meets my gaze with a giddy grin, a quick nod, and two embarrassingly enthusiastic thumbs-up. I have a feeling this is her way of congratulating me for reading my poem. And I think it might also be her way of granting permission for me to hang out with Ryan for a bit, rather than return to the bleachers to sit with her.

I have a feeling she has somehow known about him all along.

I have no idea how. Sometimes, moms just know things.

"Yeah, okay," I tell him, nodding at the exit doors. "Let's go."

There is a row of outdoor benches lined up along the gym building's wall, each one facing the seashore. The air is brisk and snappy and salt flavored. The Olympic Mountains across the water are backlit by the setting sun, the sky a vivid, glowing orange behind them. The rippling waves of Puget Sound reflect the molten light. It also catches in Ryan's hair, illuminating each golden swoop, and turning the curve of his cheek and the fringe of his eyelashes gold as he looks at me.

"Is right here okay?" he asks, gesturing at the bench.

"This is good," I say.

He nods; we sit.

He says, "This will be our school in a couple years. Hard to believe." He plucks at his bracelet again, then points off in some random direction and adds, "I live pretty close by. Just over the hill there. I grew up playing in these woods and coming down to this beach for picnics with my mom. My dad taught me how to ride my bike in the student parking lot on the weekends."

"That's cool," I say, because it is, but also because I'm not sure what else to say.

He nods again and again. "Yep. Sorry. I, um, I'm rambling—I do that when I'm nervous sometimes." His green eyes dart to me. And away. "I ramble around you a lot."

My heart slams in my chest. My entire body feels clammy and shivery. I tell him, "I've never thought so. I like our conversations."

"Me too," he says quickly. "Me too."

I swallow, trying to resist the renewed sense of hope rising up through my fingers and toes. "I'm surprised you're not wearing your new bracelet."

He pauses. Cocks his head. "What new bracelet?"

"The one from Saylor May? I heard that she asked you to Tolo with it."

"Oh. *Oh*—yeah, about that." He turns and points at another angle and says, "Okay, so, Saylor May's house is right over there, right? We grew up together. She's one of my best friends, and I've known her forever, and a few days ago, we came up with this plan for Tolo. Basically, she wanted to ask someone and make a big post about it online, *but* she was too nervous to ask the guy she really likes. And I wasn't sure if the girl that *I* really like planned to ask me. So we decided to go to the dance together, just as friends." He takes a quick breath and admits, "It was a lot less scary that way."

48

His explanation makes my heart soar. Like the seagulls squawking overhead, flapping their white wings in the sea breeze. Like the flock of huge, brown-winged and black-necked geese that just cut across the sky in a sharp V-formation.

Ryan leans in slightly and asks, "Does that make sense?"

"Yes. Yes, it does."

He gives me a shy smile. His green eyes scan my face.

The hope in my heart glows brighter and brighter.

"So, the girl you like—what can you tell me about her?"

"Well," he says. "She's really cool. Super nice. Easy to talk to. Easy to ramble to, even."

I knot my hands together in my lap to keep them from shaking.

"We met in this after-school club," he says. "But I actually saw her for the first time at the club fair in our school. I was just walking around, when I overheard these two girls arguing. And I didn't mean to eavesdrop or anything, but I saw this girl with long brown hair and heard her say, *Maybe I* will *become a mathlete.*" He snickers. Shakes his head. "I don't know why, but that was so funny to me. And I was kind of intrigued, so I watched as she stormed off. She didn't end up going to the Math Olympiad's booth; she signed up for this other club instead. It was a club for Native Americans, but when I asked the teacher in charge about it, she told me anyone could join. Everyone was welcome."

I gasp. "You—it was *you*? You were the third person in our club?"

"Yep. I added my name to the list," he says. "It was a bummer when the club was canceled, but at the same time, it all worked out okay for me.

Because the girl showed up in the other club I signed up for."

And now I'm *radiant* with hope. And disbelief. And so many feelings.

I dare to scoot an inch closer to him on the bench.

He does the same, mirroring me as he holds my gaze.

"And the powwow?" I ask. "What brought you here tonight?"

"I was at the beach with Olive earlier," he tells me. "Helping her gather seashells for some art project. And I saw the volunteers setting up for the powwow. Then I saw some flyers describing the event tonight." Ryan pauses to spin his bracelet around and around on his wrist before adding, "I didn't even know it was Indigenous Peoples' Day today. But it made me think of that day at the club fair. And it made me wonder: Will the girl I like be here? Does she go to powwows?" He shrugs a little bashfully and says, "Apparently, she does."

I can't believe it.

I can't believe my own luck.

We are seated so close to each other on the bench now. Our faces are only a few inches apart. He lifts one hand, shy and uncertain, to tuck a stray lock of windblown hair behind my ear. I lean into his touch slightly, as his fingertips graze my cheek.

He exhales. Searches my face. "Sooo . . ."

"Sooo," I echo, breaking off with a giddy little giggle.

He grins back at me. Then he stands up and offers me his hand. "So," he says. "Want to go wander around with me?"

My heart swells, and I find myself thinking of the other little poem that I wrote for today. The secret one that wasn't shared at all:

Some planets are red
Some nebulas are blue
I could spend hours
Wandering the galaxy with you

Things didn't go according to plan. But in the end, I suppose it didn't really matter.

49

My skin buzzes as Ryan and I explore the powwow together, just wandering around, holding hands. I feel electric and weightless. Like I'm a balloon, a wind sock, a wild flailing thing that has been anchored by his side.

He never lets go of my hand. He never stops smiling, either.

As we explore the powwow, we talk and talk about everything, from our favorite subjects in school to our favorite video game boss battles. We discuss our families and friends—he tells me a funny story about how he and Dante Rawlins first met, and I tell him about how I live with my mother, my grandfather, and my aunt and uncle and baby cousin.

He hesitates a moment before asking, "What about your dad?"

I shrug. "He's not really a part of my life." Ryan looks sad for me, so I quickly explain. "It's okay. I only met him once, when I was ten, and he was a total jerk. He brought up this one fight he and my mom had before I was born, and it was just so weird and unfair of him."

Ryan cringes. "Do you know what the fight was about?"

I do. It's not something I normally talk about or think about, but I feel so comfortable with Ryan right now that I decide to tell him all the details: I explain the fact that the last name Wilder comes from the Upper Skagit side of my family. My grandfather is Mac Wilder; my mother is Cadence Wilder. And when Mom found out she was expecting me, she knew immediately that she wanted me to inherit her name. Inheriting the Wilder name was important to her, especially since my blood quantum wouldn't be high enough to enroll as a citizen of the tribe. She couldn't do anything about the enrollment laws, but she felt she could at least make sure

I shared the name so other folks would know who claimed me. Whose lineage I belonged to.

For most Natives, family names and relations are far more important than blood quantum.

Chris disagreed. He believed that children should only inherit last names from their fathers, for reasons he never really made clear to my mom. She begged him to compromise; she asked if he would at least be open to hyphenating. But he argued that "Wilder" paired with his last name would be too long and awkward. He didn't like the way it sounded. He didn't like the way it would look on paper.

To this day, I am so glad and so grateful that my mother didn't stand for it.

I am proud to be Wesley Wilder.

"As you should be," Ryan reassures me. "It sounds like your mom made the right choice. Forget that guy."

"Right," I agree. "Forget him."

Eventually, after what feels like forever and hardly any time at all, Ryan checks a notification on his phone and squeezes my hand. "Ah," he says. "My mom's here to pick me up. She doesn't want me to walk home in the dark."

I nod, understanding. "Oh. Okay. So I guess I'll see you tomorrow, then?"

His green eyes meet mine, electrifying.

"Definitely," he tells me. "Do you have any plans for lunch? You should come hang out in Mr. Li's computer lab with me."

My cheeks burn with the invitation. "Actually, I'm going to be in Ms. Gilbert's classroom during lunch tomorrow. We're trying to revive the Native/Indigenous Student Union. Want to come join us?"

Ryan beams at me. "Really? Cool! Yeah, I'll be there. It'll be as if the club was never canceled at all."

"That's right," I say dreamily.

Still holding hands, we make our way through the rows of arts and crafts tables in the cafeteria and back out around the outskirts of the campus to the parking lot. Before we round the final corner and step into view, he tugs on my arm, pulling us both to a stop on the sidewalk.

"Can I give you a hug? Would that be okay?"

I smirk and nod and step into his embrace, breathing in his fresh scent. A few wisps of his golden hair tickle the side of my face. His arms are warm and firm around me. I feel his chest shudder with a jittery breath, right before he releases me.

He steps backward, his fingertips anxiously twisting his bracelet around his wrist again.

He smiles and says, "I'll see you tomorrow then."

I resist the urge to twirl and leap as I say, "Yep! See you tomorrow."

He takes one more step. "Cool. I'm looking forward to it."

"Me too."

"Enjoy the rest of your night."

"You too."

"Bye, Wesley."

"Bye, Ryan. Bye."

50

I spend the rest of the powwow floating on a cloud, and I keep on floating all the way home.

51

We get home late.

Auntie Jess and Uncle Kenji say goodnight to me; Baby Zoe fell asleep in the car and doesn't stir at all as they carry her up the stairs, off to bed. My cheeks hurt from smiling so much tonight, but I feel another little ache in my heart as I watch them go, because now I can't help but wonder how much longer we will all be here, in the same home. If they do decide to move to Tennessee, I know I want to make every single day that we have left count. I will miss them—especially Zoe—so very much if they go.

Before Grandpa goes to bed, he claps one hand on my shoulder and says, "You know, if your theory about the signal is right—I think your grandmother came by the gym tonight. I felt that urge to seek her out, while you were standing in line for the open mic. So maybe she was there. Maybe she listened, hmm?"

"Maybe she was," I agree happily.

"Humph. You did well, kiddo. I was very proud of you."

He claps my shoulder twice more, before he heads for the stairs.

Mom hugs me from behind, nuzzling my hair with her cheek. "So proud," she echoes. "So very proud of you, every single day. You're my baby girl. You're a Wilder. And you know that you belong here. Don't ever forget it. You belong. You belong. Nothing and no one will ever change that."

I place my arms over hers. "Thank you, Mom. For today. For everything."

She presses a kiss to the top of my head before she releases me.

"Hey, Mom? There's still some time left in Gemma's twenty-four-hour charity stream. Do you mind if I hang out down here for a bit to watch it?"

"Go ahead." She yawns and adds, "Just not too late, okay?"

"Not too late."

"And we're framing this, by the way," she says, holding up the copy of the newspaper that I received from Ms. Gilbert. "It's going on our wall tomorrow. Just saying."

As she climbs up the stairs, I settle onto the moss-colored couch cushions and grab the remote control. Vader hops up into my lap, purring contentedly; I scratch him behind the ears.

Then—while the TV is powering on, while the streaming app is loading—I hear it: an owl. Somewhere in the inky darkness outside, an owl is hooting. Its voice is beautiful and eerie and rhythmic and unsettling. And as I sit here, in the stillness of my quiet home, I am not sure what to make of it. Does it feel foreboding? Scary? Or does this owl sound like a guardian? A protector?

Or is it simply a nocturnal bird, announcing itself to the night?

I close my eyes, listening.

And ultimately, to me, the owl's presence feels significant but unknowable. I could try to attach some kind of meaning to it. I could call it fate. A message. An omen. I could do the same thing with so many big moments that happened today and throughout my life: Was it fate that made Skye Reynolds my lab partner? Or was it Ms. Aguilar's random selection? Was I meant to see Ella Holland dash into the girls' bathroom alone during lunch, or did our paths cross by coincidence? Did some unseen force bring Ryan Thomas to the powwow tonight? Or was it simply his sister's quest for seashells?

Looking back even further: Were Hanan and I destined to become best friends? Is there a reason why Mom and I couldn't stay in our old apartment? Was my father never meant to be a part of my life?

I could try to make sense of it all. I could try to connect the dots, the way people attempt to draw constellations in the night sky.

Or I could embrace not knowing. This world is full of mysteries. And I'm just one person, making my way through it. One wanderer in a wide-open galaxy.

But I know this much for sure: I am here. I am here. And I am ready for whatever tomorrow brings.

Author's Note

I need to begin this note with a few disclaimers:

First, as far as I know, there are no Wilder families within the Upper Skagit community. If I'm wrong and Wilders do exist, however, please note that it was never my intention to borrow anyone's likeness. These characters are not meant to represent any real Upper Skagit members or descendants. Wesley and her family are entirely fictional.

Second, blood quantum laws and membership guidelines are a sensitive topic in Indian Country. I am a tribal citizen, and I referenced my own Nation, the Upper Skagit Tribe, to contextualize these policies. I understand why the current citizenship criteria exist; blood quantum levels are widely used and supported. Meanwhile, each Indigenous Nation sets its own guidelines, taking into account such factors as ancestry, kinship, and cultural and historical ties. Tribal governments have the sovereign right to self-determination.

With that said, it's not unusual for recent descendants with family and community ties to be included in Native and First Nations social and cultural gatherings. As a mother, I hope that my tribal Nation—and others across North America—will eventually find ways to depart from blood quantum laws, which are not culturally traditional. They do not reflect Indigenous values or beliefs. Rather, they are a colonial invention. I believe we can create citizenship criteria that are better and more inclusive for our descendants. We are adaptable peoples. That is one of our greatest strengths. We can imagine future systems steeped in connection, kinship, and cultural recovery.

We are not going anywhere. We still belong here. We will always belong here. And the future generations deserve to feel that sense of belonging.

My third disclaimer: Everett, Washington, is a real city with a large public school district. However, the term "North Shore kids" is my own invention, and is not meant to reflect or stereotype any particular neighborhood or group within the city. Furthermore, Shorelands Middle School and Coastline High School are both fictional institutions. The Indigenous Peoples' Day powwow that occurs at Coastline is, by extension, a fictional event as well.

However, Coastline High School is described in a geographically specific location: it is on "the beach at the bottom of a steep bluff," overlooking the "shimmering blue waters of Puget Sound." It is described as a place where the Olympic Mountains are visible in the west, along with Whidbey, Camano, and Gedney Islands in the water, plus the Tulalip Bay to the north, and the Snohomish River to the east. This is a very real place for a very fictional high school. I intentionally chose this location because this area was the historic site of a significant Coast Salish village. It was a place where Coast Salish people lived, gathered, and traded. It was a site of commerce and diplomatic relations. And this particular region—this little corner of the Salish Sea—was known as the Land of a Thousand Fires. The area gained this nickname because the top of the bluff was once used as a lookout post. In the night, you could look out across the surrounding lands and waters and see *all* the bonfires where Coast Salish encampments were. According to some tribal historians, the bonfires were plentiful enough to almost mirror the number of stars in the sky.

Of course, in the real world, there is no high school here now. The longhouses that once stood on this beach and that lookout point on the bluff were abandoned after the Treaty of Point Elliott was signed in 1855, when Coast Salish people were forced to make difficult compromises. The Everett waterfront became industrialized through the construction of mills, railroads, and eventually a US Navy base. But this is my book. And in this fictional little universe of mine, I wanted to depict Native folks gathering directly on this coastline again.

I should note, however, that on December 10, 2014, the Everett City Council renamed the bluff as the "Hibulb Lookout." This name change was commemorated with a sign in Lushootseed; it also received a blessing from representatives of the Tulalip Tribes.

Also, the Lushootseed translation of "Indigenous Peoples' Day" in the first chapter of this book came from a calendar on the Tulalip Tribes website. Many thanks to the Tulalip Tribes Lushootseed Department, for making so many free resources available online.

Lastly, in June 2021, I participated in a Books

for Palestine auction. This auction was hosted by folks in the children's literature community, and all of the funds raised from our donations went to the Middle East Children's Alliance, as well as the Palestine Children's Relief Fund. As a donor to this cause, I offered readers the opportunity to name a character in my next book. I would like to thank Drew D. for supporting Palestinian children and for choosing the name Ryan Thomas!

Acknowledgments

This book was written during the COVID-19 pandemic. While I created the earliest outlines of Wesley's story, a field hospital was erected in the neighborhood where I grew up, just down the street from my parents' house. While I worked on this story about a gamer girl with a crush, set over the course of one big day in her young life, school buildings were closed all around the world. While I stayed home, relatively safe with my newborn daughter as well as a newborn draft of this book, millions of essential citizens and workers continued to show up for others.

In her fantastic book *Big Magic: Creative Living Beyond Fear*, Elizabeth Gilbert writes, "What we make matters enormously, and it doesn't matter at all." As a creative professional who has now lived through a historic global health crisis, I am astonished by the truth of this phrase. Because, of course, I hope this book matters. I hope it will matter enormously to my young readers in particular.

But at the end of the day, *We Still Belong* is just a book. It is a collection of pages bound together. It is black text on white paper. It is my hard work, as well as my heart work; and I hope this story will resonate, that kids will connect with Wesley and her friends and her family. But no matter how far this book goes, it will only ever be a work of fiction. A daydream in print. A moment of make-believe.

There is great value in fiction. But there is much greater value to be found in the real world, in the concrete ways that people work together, support each other, and provide for one another. One might argue that art is essential in our society, but it will never be as vital as our need for agriculture, or medicine, or ecological restoration. Artists will never provide services as crucial as postal workers, or emergency responders, or early childhood educators. There are scientists in the world right now who are developing biodegradable materials to replace plastic packaging and renewable energy technologies to help us achieve carbon neutrality. There are volunteer search and rescue teams whose actions and bravery save lives.

There are plenty of people out there whose contributions to our society matter much more than what I could ever hope to offer as an author. Which is why I must acknowledge all of you first: the teachers, the nurses, the engineers, the wastewater treatment plant operators, the machinists and fabricators, the cargo and warehouse workers, the grocery store and food service employees, the culture keepers and community gardeners, among countless others. Thank you for the work you do. You build the world. You bring it all together.

Furthermore: I must express my deepest gratitude, once again, to my editorial dream team. Rosemary Brosnan, you understand me and my work and my heart so well. Thank you for helping me grow as a writer, and for helping me keep track of the timelines and chapter numbers and vehicle descriptions in each manuscript. (In a rough draft of *We Still Belong*, Wesley's mom drove a beige station wagon, which somehow miraculously transformed into a green Jeep later in the story. No one knows how or why. But I went with the Jeep.) Cynthia Leitich Smith (Muscogee), your thoughtful notes and feedback and encouragement always lift me up. Courtney Stevenson, you know how to describe my books better than I do. Jill Amack and Mikayla Lawrence (Cowlitz), I am so grateful for your work on Wesley's story. Thank you all. I am eternally grateful for everything that you do for me and my characters and their journeys.

Additional thanks go to everyone else at HarperCollins/Heartdrum. I must express particularly huge, heartfelt thanks to Patty, Mimi, Katie, Christina, and Stephanie—the school and library marketing team. For most middle grade authors, schools and libraries are our bread and butter. Your educational resources, promotional campaigns, and recommendations have been instrumental to the foundation of my career. Thank you for believing in Edie, Maisie, and now Wesley. I also need to thank Madelyn Goodnight (Chickasaw) for capturing the heart and soul of this story so gorgeously on the cover. I love absolutely everything about it. Additional thanks go to Celeste Knudsen for her incredible design work. You two made this book beautiful, inside and out.

I am very grateful for my literary agent, Suzie Townsend, for her smart guidance and reassuring presence. Thank you for helping me reach new and unimaginable heights as an author. My immense gratitude also goes to Suzie's assistants, Sophia Ramos and Kendra Coet, as well as everyone else at New Leaf Literary & Media, Inc. Thank you for the enthusiasm you have shown for my work over the years.

I need to acknowledge the Upper Skagit Indian

Tribe, especially the current members of the Upper Skagit Tribal Council, and the tribe's steadfast employees, who have all made a huge difference in my life. I am so proud to be Upper Skagit. And I am so grateful to our tribal leaders for their prompt, community-focused response to the COVID-19 pandemic. Your organization and attentiveness demonstrated true leadership in a tumultuous time. Tigwicid.

I also want to thank the independent bookstores who carry my work. No algorithms will ever compare to bookseller recommendations. No virtual retailers will ever capture the magic of a lovingly curated bookstore. Thank you for serving your communities. And for advocating for the freedom to read.

As always, I am so grateful for my family members. All of you.

I am especially grateful for my husband, Mazen. I'm grateful for your humor, your intelligence, and your endlessly caring heart. Thank you for being a wonderful husband and father. Thank you for working hard and showing up for us, every single day. I love you very much.

And to my daughter, Mia: I love you so much, it scares me sometimes. But oh, what a privilege it is to feel that fear. From the moment you came into my life, you have brought more joy, more love, more wonder, more of everything into sharp relief for me. I am grateful to be your mother. It is a privilege to watch you grow up and to help guide you through this wild and mysterious life. I am an imperfect person, and I know I won't always be right; I will probably make many mistakes along the way. I am still learning and growing, just like you. Just like everyone. But I promise to keep an open heart, and an open mind, and an endless supply of love for you. I am here. I am here. And no matter what the future brings, this will always be true.

I am right here for you.

A Note from Cynthia Leitich Smith, Author-Curator of Heartdrum

Dear Reader,

One of the bravest things you can do is open your heart. It doesn't always work out like you'd hope, and that can hurt your feelings—like when Wesley's teacher failed to appreciate her poem about Indigenous Peoples' Day. But it can be surprising in a good way, like when Wesley offered emotional support to Ella and they became friends. And it can make you feel like you're riding a roller coaster of awkwardness, like when Wesley tried to let Ryan know she *liked him* liked him, and when he let her know that he *liked her* liked her, too.

Author Christine Day doesn't promise that you'll never feel rejected. But through Wesley, she shows what it means to move through an uncertain world with a courageous heart.

Have you read many stories by and about Native

people? Two of my favorites are also by Christine Day: *I Can Make This Promise* and *The Sea in Winter*. Like *We Still Belong*, these novels are published by Heartdrum, a Native-focused imprint of HarperCollins Children's Books, which offers stories about young Indigenous heroes by Native and First Nations authors and illustrators. I'm honored to publish this book because it's written with tenderness and compassion, because Wesley is so full of hope, and because anyone with a cat named Vader sounds like a lot of fun.

More personally, this story is a love letter to the children of tribal members who value, honor, and respect their Indigenous cultural heritage. Wesley says you belong, and I'll go a step further: you are dearly loved.

Mvto,

Cynthia Leitich Smith